Praise for the novels of Thomas Moran

THE WORLD I MADE FOR HER

"Moran relates the nightmarish predicament of his empathic characters in hypnotic prose that remains compelling right up until the final scene. . . . [His] poetic, cruel yet forgiving love story will not easily be forgotten."
—*Publishers Weekly*

"Fast-paced, filled with vivid human detail, and deeply affecting."
—*Kirkus Reviews*

"Moran knows full well that when the body is under duress the mind becomes susceptible to occult whispers—some discomforting, others soothing, and all suggestive of an immaterial reality that any good skeptic struggles to refute." —*The New York Times Book Review*

"A reading experience as fresh and basic as lying down feverish on cool, clean linens with loving hands to tuck you in." —*Time*

"Imagine *The English Patient* taking place in a New York City hospital, and you'll get a sense of Thomas Moran's *The World I Made for Her*. . . . Astonishingly adept at keeping you interested in a character who can neither move nor speak—let alone act on his feelings—this provocative novel . . . celebrates the fact that, wherever it finds us, love is mostly lived out in the mind." —*Glamour*

THE MAN IN THE BOX
Winner of Book-of-the-Month Club's
Stephen Crane Award for First Fiction

"As in the diary of Anne Frank, the blend of confinement, sexual awakening, and cruelty in this novel makes for a potent and unblinking coming-of-age tale." —*The New Yorker*

"We hear the echoes of other Holocaust literature. From Jerzy Kosinski and Elie Wiesel through Cynthia Ozick . . ." —*Los Angeles Times*

"Attached to every instance of altruism, bound up with every amiable affectionate or romantic impulse in this novel, are the beasts of prejudice and self-gratification. It is as if Moran had turned *Schindler's List* on its head." —*The New York Times Book Review*

"Moran knows that the human impulse toward good is not unmixed. The grip of a strong narrative and characters presented with a full range of capacities, including jealousy and betrayal, impart the throb of real life to *The Man in the Box*."

—Pearl Abraham, author of *The Romance Reader*

ALSO BY THOMAS MORAN

The Man in the Box

THE WORLD I MADE FOR HER

THOMAS MORAN

RIVERHEAD BOOKS
NEW YORK

RIVERHEAD BOOKS
Published by The Berkley Publishing Group
A division of Penguin Putnam Inc.
375 Hudson Street
New York, New York 10014

This is a work of fiction. Names, characters, places, and incidents
either are the products of the author's imagination or are used
fictitiously, and any resemblance to actual persons, living or dead,
events, or locales is entirely coincidental.

First Riverhead hardcover edition: June 1998
First Riverhead trade paperback edition: June 1999
Riverhead trade paperback ISBN: 1-57322-731-5

The Penguin Putnam Inc. World Wide Web site address is
http://www.penguinputnam.com

The Library of Congress has catalogued the Riverhead hardcover edition as follows:

Moran, Thomas.
The world I made for her / by Thomas Moran.
p.   cm.
ISBN 1-57322-084-1 (acid-free paper)
1. Irish Americans—New York (State)—New York—Fiction.
I. Title.
PS3563.07714W67   1998   97-46699 CIP
813.'54—dc21

Printed in the United States of America

10   9   8   7   6   5   4   3   2   1

With thanks to
Wendy Carlton,
Jane Dystel,
and Miriam Goderich

IN MEMORY OF BRUNO VOGRIG

"There is time, if you need the comfort, to touch the person next to you . . ."

—THOMAS PYNCHON

THE WORLD I MADE
FOR HER

1

I KNEW SOMEONE NAMED NUALA. Nuala means "white shoulders" in Irish, but no one much remembers these old things anymore, not even in west Ireland. Nuala's parents spoke no Irish. Yet Nial and Maire Riordan were in love with the sound of that ancient name. They began saying it every day as soon as Maire became pregnant, though they did not know whether the creature in her belly was a girl or a boy. They had the habit of talking directly to Nuala inside Maire's swelling stomach. They were that sure.

Nuala did not disappoint them. The name suited her from the moment she left the womb, which she did with scarcely a tear or wail just before one of those rare Irish dawns when the sun slipped up over the horizon undimmed by fog banks or clouds.

Nuala's father thought that bright light was a dicey omen. The relative degrees of the sun's obscurity and the type of rain at the time of birth had specific meanings, at least in the augeries of the old folks. There was always prophesy in the weather at a birth. But an open sun at dawn? Who could be sure of anything so unusual? The wisest crones kept their opinions to themselves. From birth, there was always an uncertainty about Nuala Riordan.

Today, Nuala can count the number of people she's disappointed in her life on the fingers of one hand. The ones she knows of for sure, anyway. She doubts there are any secret ones lurking about. She's very proud of this, considering she's already twenty-eight years old, has seen a bit of life, and has her own green card, which she's earned through her profession. She's not like the Irish who sneak into America on tourist visas; staying in the Irish neighborhoods of Queens, working nonunion construction jobs or tending bars in which the bitterness of failed dreams billows thick as the blue clouds of cigarette smoke.

She's had five boyfriends. The last romance seemed full of promise, until he was killed. Her grief is still too young to behave itself, so she never lets it out.

Nuala's small, not above five and a half feet. Her shoulders are thin but broad, like a young boy's, and creamy white where I've glimpsed them. So is her face. She has green eyes that are too large and make her look startled even when she isn't. I don't believe Nuala's been truly startled very many times in her life. She can probably count the occasions on the fingers of one hand.

Nuala glows for me on rainy days. She's just luminous.

It's because rain is her natural element, I think. Never mind the strange clarity of her birth. Where Nuala comes from, it's a thin sun that ever shines. But there are three or four types of misting, at least four kinds of fog, and perhaps six or seven different rains. Where Nuala's from, they identify precipitation as discreetly as the Eskimos do snow. Nuala laughs at what people here call cloudbursts or showers or drizzles. She knows those terms are not subtle enough to mean anything about what's coming from the heavens.

Her hair is reddish brown and would be wild as bush if she didn't tame it with barrettes and rubber bands. Her hair's gorgeous. I've heard a lot of women say so, and they're the only honest judges. But Nuala's not beautiful. She's just a regular girl, though she has lovely thick straight eyebrows and her features all fit well together. On certain days in certain lights, she's pretty enough to fall in love with. But you'd have to be able to handle that Nuala is always Nuala in any light; she has no fear of storms or of the dark. "To hell with you," she'll say when she feels like it, and she'll really mean it for that moment. She's not one to let any slight or any ignorance pass unremarked.

She reminds me of a certain Balthus painting I can never get out of my head. It's the one of the girl Balthus later married, who refused to remove her brassiere when posing because she didn't want her breasts displayed in a museum anywhere. But eventually when I'm able to tell Nuala this, she just laughs and says I ought to take an art history course. "I look like none in the wide world but myself," Nuala says.

One day I'd like to find a picture of someone in a magazine who looks exactly like her, just to see her frown and deny there's any resemblance.

If you had any heart at all, you'd be pleased to hear Nuala call your name. You'd be very happy if Nuala were one day to fall in love with you. You'd think her da was dead wrong when he worried about the omen of the sun on the day of her birth. You'd bless the day.

You'd feel fond of the damp, misty Ireland that made Nuala the woman she is today. You'd thank her mother for teaching her soft ways; and the nuns in her school, who were cruel and kindhearted at the same time; and her granddad, who took her out fishing in his curragh when she was wee and made her fearless.

I SEE NUALA about three days a week. She's an early arriver; she likes to set up her tasks and prepare mentally for all she'll have to do during her shift. We never exchange many words, because her work is so utterly different from mine. She's one of the active ones. I'm just an observer in most of the procedures; other things I do all alone. We are very aware of each other, though. There are twelve like me when the Unit is full, and six like Nuala and Brigit, and others who come and go, circulating from room to room to room as they're needed. A few of them act like real friends. Brigit, for instance, is easy to get on with. She's always got something to tell you; many things happen to her in her private life that she likes to relate. But I can hardly get Nuala to smile at me, she's so serious. Some of us tease her, especially Brigit. "Lighten up, Nualala, you frustrated virgin," Brigit'll say. Something like that will make Nuala smile; she's affectionate with Brigit, who's Irish too. To the rest of us, Nuala is reserved, but equally, so she's not resented for it. And when she does at least smile and say a few words, she favors everyone equally.

I spend more time than I should watching Nuala move around the room at her scientific tasks. I like the shape of her legs; they're thin and thin-thighed, but there's a pleasing bulge of muscle on her calves. I've gotten to examine her hands pretty closely when we've done one or two things together. They're ideal, if you're someone who appreciates hands. The two wrist bones are well defined, the hands themselves are long and slender, and her fingers taper nicely and not too sharply, which can give a girl a sinister appearance as you know. No, Nuala's hands are beyond reproach.

If you had any heart at all, you'd be pleased if one day Nuala were to stroke your face.

Now generally you know you are on the way to emotional trouble when you begin to think seriously on a woman's hands, especially when you've already been admiring her legs and in particular appreciating her ankles. But I'm not worrying. This is an unusual time for me; I'm not engaged in these things the way I might ordinarily be. Let's just say for now that circumstances have temporarily limited my fields of vision, and Nuala is the most striking person who comes into range. I do think Nuala is one of life's special ones, and I hope that she likes me.

Meanwhile, we all have our jobs to do. It's serious work we're engaged in—twenty-four hours, day in, day out. It's important to check and recheck; you can't let anything slide or go undone because everything has a schedule. But I do have time on my hands, a few circumstances beyond my control. So I begin to construct a gift for Nuala in my mind.

Nuala. Not Brigit.

Brigit's much prettier; she has the air of proprietorship everywhere she goes. You know this type of woman. She's confident. She acts sure she belongs wherever she is, and she gives an impression of wondering about the rest of us. "I just don't know what you're doing here," she's said to me, not meanly, but not entirely joking either. "Really, it's inexcusable that you haven't moved on after all this time. You're a slacker, you are. A slouch, sure."

Brigit doesn't know that I've seen the tiny punctures of pediatric hypodermics in the fine webs of skin between her fingers. Something is going into Brigit that she knows ought not to be. She's doing it, but she's hiding it. She knows it's dangerous. I feel I am sharing a sort of secret life with her, aware as I am of her danger, but she doesn't know it yet. I want to talk to her about it, but it's not possible just now.

Brigit moves in this world so easily. Nuala moves cautiously as a tough but mistreated cat, eyes wide open for trouble. Part of it may be her grief. Part, I think, is that she feels she doesn't really belong; she feels separate and unknown. She's never afraid, just alert and ready to move fast if she has to.

In the world I would make for Nuala, there would be someone to whom she could tell her greatest secret without a single thought of betrayal.

In the world I would make, she would be light as a feather when she arose from her bed and always feel freshly washed. She would have the simple things that comfort her: an alpaca throw to put over her legs when she's reading, maybe a cat or a parrot for company. No takeout Chinese food; decent meals cooked at home. Plenty of hot water for her bath in the morning, and radiator pipes that don't bang like cracked old bronze church bells in the middle of the night.

In the world I would make, no one would ever again die in her arms.

In the world I would make for Nuala, she would finally arrive at a place that was always there, empty and waiting only for her.

2

THE FIRST THING WE WANT TO KNOW anywhere we are: What is the weather in this place? Will our days be full of sunshine or rain? Our nights dank, or crisp and starlit?

What a useless pursuit. Here, it is always exactly the same temperature, the light is the constant precise glow of the fluorescents hanging from the ceilings. You need to enter a conspiracy with Brigit to get one of the windows open.

You have to understand that I check in and I check out. When I'm gone, they say I'm in a coma. "He's here again!" Brigit shouts when I check back in. "And what did you see, love?" she always asks me. Most of the time: nothing. Most of the time it is black and timeless. But on three or four occasions, I have not only seen things, I've lived them. And I try so hard to tell her, I want someone to know what it's like. But I fail. I can't control my right hand enough to write.

And I can't talk.

I have a hole in the base of my throat the size of an egg, and it's plugged with a valve attached to a thick plastic tube. It's a pale blue umbilical cord that keeps me alive. It connects me to the ventilator, which does my breathing for me. The only intermediary is a small gray box with little lights and switches near my bed. The blue tubing just goes right through it and into the wall. Somewhere in that wall is my hidden source of oxygen, and life. The nurses call it "The Machine." It makes it seem as if the entire hospital building is The Machine, breathing in its gigantic mechanical way from some mysterious center to keep us all alive.

Whether we want to be or not.

I'm not sure yet about myself. I feel sometimes I have been on the very edge of death, and pulled back in horror. Other times I am sure I have been dead for a short time and found it a relief, only to be brought back by The Machine and the hypodermic needles they ram into my diminishing veins.

Whenever I check back in on Nuala's shift, she comes and stares at me. Her huge green eyes are on mine, I can see her irises dilate. She looks for the longest time without moving or saying a thing. Maybe she's trying to see if I've brought back any secrets from the other side. Then suddenly she will break eye contact and briskly adjust my ventilator tubing, and the two or three intravenous drips in my arms, the one in my neck, the pulse meter on my thumb, the thin tube that runs from my nose all the way down to my stomach. Every time they change the liquid food in that tube, I can actually taste it, although this is physically impossible. Mostly it's like vanilla milk shakes. Once or twice a day, something orange and peppery is added.

Sometimes when I first check back in I'm confused. I have no idea where I am or what state I'm in. I only know it is unnatural. So I slowly pull the feeding tube all the way up from my stomach and out of my nose. It takes a while. The tube is so long, and it feels so odd to be pulling something so long out of yourself. Then I go to work on the intravenous tubes. Usually Brigit or Nuala or one of the others catches me by then. They get cross. They tie my hands to the rails of the bed with strips of white cotton.

I think, *The bad girls have tied me down again.* I make faces at them, hoping they will understand my question: Why are you doing this to me?

My secret plan is that when I have finished making a world for Nuala, that is where I will go when I finally check out. Because some of the places I go now are terrible.

TWELVE PATIENTS, six nurses: that's the population of our Intensive Care Unit. Patients can't get to know one another because none of us can speak; we're all connected to The Machine or are comatose. And no one is mobile, we can't move from our private rooms. I don't want to know them anyway. They're all dying, I think. How could I die? I'm not even halfway through my thirties, and I have always looked younger than my age. I feel like a contemporary of Brigit and Nuala, though I wouldn't be surprised if they thought I was too old, say, for them to consider dating. Of course that's problematical in other ways as well. I have been here for a long time now, and I have not seen myself in a mirror once. They don't allow mirrors here. Probably they don't want you to be shocked by the way you've changed.

When you arrive at the state I'm in, you have to face it. You are no longer normal. And neither is your mind. In addition to whatever virus is corroding and rotting your body and brain, there are the drugs. So many drugs, some of them very heavy duty, like fentanyl, which makes morphine seem like Children's Tylenol. I get antiulcer medication, anticonvulsants, and grand mixes of the newest antibiotics, some in combinations never used on a patient before. And, every evening, a needle full of anticlotting agents in the stomach.

I am a masterpiece of plumbing. Small plastic valves are inserted into my veins and taped in place, so that each change in intravenous medication doesn't require punching a new hole in me. Of course these valves are not permanent and must be moved every week or so. The only permanent hole is my trache; the only permanent tube is my catheter. Yet I am always sprouting tubes everywhere. And there are the leg bags, which inflate and deflate on a regular basis to keep my blood moving while I'm supine.

Frequently I think of myself as a science project, or an experimental animal in a research lab. Except that some days I am sharp enough to recognize worry in the doctors' eyes when some new strategy doesn't appear to be working. Doctors are professionals. They want successful conclusions; they do not want to fail. Sometimes I think I can smell their fear of failure. They are trying to save me but aren't sure they can.

Someone is almost always within sight of me, and I'm wired with as many alarms as a museum. Someone would come to help me in seconds, if I needed help. But I do feel abandoned on those early evenings when Nuala comes to check all my drips or give me my last shot. Sometimes she'll smooth the blankets over my chest with her perfect hands. But as she says good night, it's rare that she'll look me in the eyes and give me a smile. I worry a little that in my illness I've become repulsive.

Or maybe I'm another hopeless case, and Nuala's had enough of those already in her life.

I hear Brigit across the hall. "Don't you worry, Mrs. Petacci. You'll sleep tonight. I've given you enough to make an elephant sleep, for Jesus' sake." Mrs. Petacci is in a semivegetative state, but when she wakes she always complains that she never gets any sleep. So Brigit tells her things like that even when she's about as conscious as a potato. Brigit believes that most patients in comas are registering what they hear in their deep subconscious, so she talks to them exactly as if they were awake.

Once when I was checked out, I thought I heard Brigit's voice from very far away saying, "Who's that hard-on for? Is it for me?"

BRIGIT AND NUALA usually leave the hospital together when their shift ends, about eight, and walk down the streets of Greenwich Village to the Bells of Hell for a beer. It's an Irish bar but mostly draws hospital people, never the Hell's Kitchen types. Nuala and Brigit learned to avoid them very quickly when they arrived in New York.

I know the place from before. I reckon Nuala and Brigit always sit at the bar and talk to Peter, the bartender. He's English. Whenever no one is playing the jukebox, he goes over and drops a coin for "No Future," by the Sex Pistols. The song's at least ten years out of date, but no one can persuade him to remove it. He says, "Brigit, how many did you croak today?" And she always laughs and says, "Oh, about a dozen. Wait'll your liver starts to crumble like an old sponge. We'll get you in there for your last days. No good drugs for you. We'll make you taste some real pain."

"Ah, Brigit, you'll break my heart long before my liver goes. The prettiest girl in New York, and you won't have a thing to do with me, just because I'm English. I cry myself to sleep every night."

"You pass out every night," Brigit says. I'd bet she's radiating sex. She just does it to torment the poor bastard. "All you'd do if I let you into my bed is snore."

Nuala sips her Guinness, a little smile on her lips. She's in love with Brigit's spirit. She wishes she could be more like her. Except that she wouldn't want to sleep with as many men as Brigit does. There's a new one almost every week—a few of them doctors, but most not; Brigit finds doctors too cold. It's trouble for sure, Nuala thinks. Not just the diseases so much as the personal exposure.

Waking up next to someone you've never woke up next to before is a frightening thing. Nuala has to feel very comfortable with a man, very familiar. She doesn't like the thrill of the new; she doesn't like the slight hint of danger. She's shared her bed with no one for more than twelve months now. Some nights she feels tormented, she wants so much for someone to touch her. Others she feels she could easily be a nun, no regrets.

The interns and residents, and everyone else at the Bells of Hell, know enough to leave Nuala alone. But when Nuala goes home, almost always before midnight, Brigit goes to the girls' room for a few minutes, comes out looking electric, and stays for one more Guinness. Someone almost always slides into the seat next to her.

"Sorry I'm late," she jokes to one man who has taken Nuala's stool before Brigit has made it back from the girls'.

"At least you've come," he says.

"More than most women can hope for," she says, and they collapse laughing. Peter scowls, then goes off to play the Sex Pistols on the juke.

And there's me, wide awake in the ward, lying perfectly flat with my needle-studded arms at my sides. My body is so atrophied I can scarcely move. It's a feat to raise my right arm high enough to scratch my nose. They give me things to help me sleep but I've got too much tolerance for them now, and they are very stingy about raising doses. The fentanyl drip doesn't really do it either. It kicks in at intervals they've designed to keep the pain in my chest bearable.

This is one of my clearheaded nights. It's tedious. There's a big clock on the opposite wall, so I'll always know what time it is. What brain surgeon had that idea? I'd like to kill him. The clock makes the night lonelier, articulating the passing of each quarter hour. I'd like to tell someone to take it down or turn it to the wall, but I can't.

So I imagine Nuala walking home from the Bells of Hell. She lives just a few blocks away in a one-bedroom on the top floor of a five-story walk-up. The landlord's cheap and has fluorescent lights in the hallway, so it always looks cold and greenish. I can see Nuala's fine ankles rising out of her white nurses' shoes and the movement of the rounded muscles in her calves as she takes each step.

She opens her door. It's dark inside. She turns on the light in the kitchen, has a look in the refrigerator. Nothing much to see. She turns off the kitchen light, walking in the darkness to her bedroom. She turns on the light by the bed, takes off her uniform and her underwear, and she puts on some gray flannel pajamas her mother sent her from Ireland. She walks to the bathroom and brushes her teeth while she sits on the toilet and pees. She looks at her face in the mirror while she washes her hands afterward.

Then she pads back across the living room and slips into bed. She sleeps on white Irish linen sheets, which she loves. It is her biggest luxury, these sheets. She starts to read a book by a Frenchman—*A Very Long Engagement*—but soon she is in tears. She turns out the light and cries herself to sleep.

In the world I'm making for Nuala, she would have a hand to hold beneath the sheets and no reason to cry over a French novel.

3

IN THE ICU, they usually don't trouble much about your name, since almost everyone passes out of their hands within a week. Most of them die. But after I'd been there awhile, Brigit decided to take a closer look at my chart. She saw that while my last name, Blatchley, was clearly of English origin, my middle name was Synge. This excited her right away.

"Family name, isn't it? Your mother's side were Synges, from south of Dublin, right?" she said.

I nodded yes.

"So you're bloody Irish too, James Synge Blatchley. Why didn't you say so? We're much nicer to the Irish than anyone else," Brigit said, laughing. "Don't blame your da for snitching a Synge. They have a reputation as dark beauties. But high spirited, not taking to the bit at all."

I nodded yes again, and both she and Nuala burst into laughter.

"And we thought you were just another scurvy Anglo-Saxon. I'm surprised you don't have a first name like Clive or Simon," said Nuala.

"You're half one of us. Like a half brother. When did your folks come over? The Famine?"

I'd discovered in my solitary hours that I could shape words with my mouth, though no sound ever came. It's that way for everyone with a trache. But the nurses had to be excellent lip-readers, I figured. They must have had so much practice, patient after dying patient trying to tell them things. It was an effort I'd not yet made. But now I tried mouthing nineteen sixteen. It didn't go over very well. "When the rats left the ship," Nuala said. "Well, never mind, you weren't even born yet. Been back?"

I shook my head no. Grandda Synge was going to be hanged by the English after the Easter Rebellion, so he fled. He was no rat, just a republican. That was too much to try, just now. But I felt elated, thinking Nuala had "heard" me at last.

"All right, Mr. James Synge from Dublin Blatchley, that's a fine credential, and so we're your new friends," Brigit said. "But right now we've most reluctantly got to do something that may seem over-intimate between new friends. They put a Texas condom on you when you first came in to keep you from wetting your bed, and now we've got to put in a more permanent device. Unless you like wetting your bed every night, which we don't believe you do, being half-Irish and not the watery Englishman we thought you were."

They pulled down my bedclothes and lifted my gown before I could even blink. Nuala gently took my penis, stretched it out straight a bit farther than I was aware it could go, and with her forefingers pulled open the hole at the tip. Brigit immediately inserted a lubricated plastic tube that looked way too wide to me and began pushing it in quarter-inch by quarter-inch, until it felt as though the damn thing had gone all the way to my balls. But aside from a creepy sensation inside where the tube was moving, there wasn't much feeling. Certainly it never felt like two pretty girls were playing with my prick. It was over in a minute or two. They covered me right back up and plugged my tube to a bag that hung by a hook to the side of the bed.

"The idea," Brigit explained, "is that you just pee whenever the hell you feel like it, even if you're asleep or going under on drugs, and it all goes very neatly into this bag, which some poor sod will have to change on a regular basis.

"And we're just going to sit here for a while to see that you do pee and everything's shipshape," Nuala said. "Some men are a little intimidated by it at first, because it does feel like you're wetting yourself when you've nothing to aim at, not even a beer bottle on a long car trip."

Brigit and Nuala are having a fine time with me. Their spirits are so good. They check my IVs, my various drips, my drug dosages in the chart. "Hope you've got good insurance, buster," Brigit says as she prepares a Valium injection. I'm sure they think I'll go all warm and biddable on the dose, but the drug does nothing and after ten minutes I still haven't peed.

I felt embarrassed. I was wondering, sick as I was, if they'd thought my dick was an acceptable size. Trained nurses have seen a couple of thousand, no doubt, and I'm concerned about how I measure up. What I really needed was some antipsychotic medication.

"Not so bad, was it?" Brigit said, as if she'd read my mind. "A fine one like that always makes it easier."

"Couldn't have slid in easier," Nuala added. "Used up a great length of the tube, though."

Clearly this was a routine they went through frequently with selected patients about whom they'd made some judgment as to their tolerance for teasing.

I still didn't have to pee.

After thirty minutes Nuala left to handle one of her other patients. Brigit kept sitting. She was studying my face. "I'm trying to figure out what you look like without the pox. It's almost gone, but it's still amazingly hard to tell. You'd look like a scabby medieval beggar if we draped some really filthy rags over you. Anyway, tell me, who's this Clare who shows up so much? Not a wife. Lover? No? Sister? Yes? Ah, I don't believe ya. There's more there than that."

After an hour, the resident in charge came by. He looked at my chart, and at the empty urine bag. "Don't you feel like having a good pee? You know, pisssssssssssssssss, pisssssssssss."

No reaction from me. I was trying to decide, from what I had seen of Brigit's round little body, whether she ought to try to lose five pounds or ten.

The resident checked all my drips and my feeding tubes. "He's getting plenty. I'd like to know where he's keeping it. I don't want his bladder bursting on my shift. Come get me in a half hour if he still hasn't peed," he said to Brigit.

"Doctor, maybe his thing's too big. Why, you should have seen the size of that monster!" Brigit said.

The resident blushed. "I don't know where you get your sense of humor, Brigit."

After another half hour, I was feeling like I had to let go. Brigit left the room to get the resident. As soon as she did, I tried relaxing all my muscles. Nothing happened. I felt that awkwardness about wetting myself. But then it came in a warm rush, and pretty soon the bag was three-quarters full and foaming.

The resident took one look and patted Brigit on the back. "I knew you'd get him to do it somehow. You tickle him, or tell him Irish jokes?"

"Get out of here," Brigit said, and he did.

Nuala came back, and they prepared me for the night. I began to feel frightened, as I always did at the winding down of the day. They adjusted my fentanyl drip and injected more Valium to help me stay calm and sleep. They tucked the covers up to my chin, but left my well-plumbed arms on top. They handed me over to the night nurses.

When they said good night, I was always looking for something in Nuala's eyes, some expression that would comfort me. But she just seemed like a girl who'd put in a hard day's work and was looking forward to a drink.

IN THOSE EARLY WEEKS, Nuala only showed one single sign of personal interest. She was intrigued by the graceful black tattoo on the inside of my left forearm. It consists of four elaborate Chinese characters, done by an ancient man in Hong Kong, who was as much a master calligrapher as a tattooist, even if most of his clients now were Marines.

"What's it mean? I've seen nothing like it," Nuala said one day while searching for a good vein to tap with her steel needle.

I wanted to tell her in Mandarin—not that I spoke it, but I had memorized my tattoo. I thought it would impress her to hear it in Chinese, help make her think I might be something more interesting than another helpless patient in critical condition.

But I can't speak. So I mouth, clearly as I can: The soul in winter dreams of the rising sun. She looks puzzled, so I try again, very slowly, and I see understanding in her face.

"Very poetic, Mr. Blatchley," Nuala said solemnly. Was it a sheen of tears in her eyes I noticed then, or just a play of the light that made them glisten?

"And what if someone's winter never ends?" she asked. "What if someone's whole life is cold and dark? What does the soul do then?"

4

IT'S NUALA WHO WAKES ME every morning and
tries to put me to sleep every evening. Or at least she
does the three or four days each week she's on duty.
Otherwise it's someone else, and those days are not
as good. I'm more likely to check out on one of those
days. Nobody's noticed this pattern. And there's nothing anyone could do if they did. Nuala couldn't be my
personal nurse, seven days a week. It'd be impossible.

But I feel I go with Nuala all day and all night,
even when I don't see her. I hold her in my mind, and
she carries me, though she doesn't know it. I'm glad
of that, for I don't want to be a burden to her. I've
somehow got the idea that I can help her.

My mind can't always hold, though. Things are
happening to my mind that make me weep. I fight and

fight but there's always the bony face of death, staring at me with hollow eyes. It's not personal; I understand that. It's not my own death. It's the death that has already taken my grandfather, my father, my friends Roger and Bruno and Eddie. They're gone, so gone, and I don't know where to look for them.

Brigit always comes to me when she sees I am crying. She can't know why, and I can't tell her. But within her loud Irish pleasure at being alive she harbors an understanding, I think, of how things can look from the other side, though she never sees it herself. Brigit holds my hand and looks in my eyes. That's all. She doesn't say anything; she doesn't try to chaff or cheer me. She just holds my hand with her cool, soft hand until the tears stop. Then she smiles at me and goes on with her duties.

So, calmer, I lie there and hear my every breath. Moisture collects in the blue oxygen tube, and when it reaches a certain level, it rattles and bubbles. Sometimes it's hypnotic, proof of my existence. Sometimes it drives me mad. I imagine the whole world, breathing in and out in an exact, controlled rhythm, the bubbling life of the world, the world itself The Machine.

And what if The Machine has AIDS? I don't, but there are people I know who do. There are people I know who've died of it. There is even a girl I know dying of it now in another ward. Suppose the world itself is the carrier of this plague? Will all of us get it then, sooner or later? How will I make a safe place for Nuala then? No, these are only fever thoughts. And I can see by the monitor that my blood oxygen levels are falling. When they fall far enough, alarms will go off, nurses and doctors will rush to my bed, they'll adjust The Machine, the fentanyl and anticonvulsants. If it's bad, a surgeon will come and slice a small hole in my right chest wall. They'll ram a stainless steel tube into my chest, and they'll suction out globs of bloody mucus. I hate the smell of it. They have to move fast; the cut will be quick and ugly and leave a ragged scar. A war souvenir, if I survive. But, after all, I'm not a pretty girl whose young body shouldn't be marred more than is absolutely necessary. My mouth will open in a scream no one will hear when the scalpel slices between my ribs.

But then most likely I'll check out for a while. It's not quite like falling asleep. It's more the sudden blackness of anesthesia. It lacks the peace of drifting into sleep; it lacks the prospect of pleasant dreams. It simply seizes you. You're gone, instantly.

I see Nuala by the bed now. I wish just once she'd place her hand against my cheek and whisper, "Don't go. Stay with me."

They never know if I'm coming back, you see. Nobody knows.

THIS TIME I'm in a big ward on a very high floor of a hospital in a city I don't know. The world outside's gray with rain; the big river that curves through the city below us is dreary and flat. But I'm not in bed. I'm on my feet; I can walk. I'm wearing a white coat and have a stethoscope draped around my neck. A black Jamaican woman who is an orderly in my real room is with me, but here she's a nurse. Over every bed there is a television, and in the beds occupied by old people the TVs are all tuned to game shows. The volume is deafening. I ask the nurse to go around and lower the sound. She's says it has to be that loud or the patients won't be able to hear it. *God*, I think, *how can they bear this noise?* There's a doctor with me who resembles Brigit, but she's too serious. "Let's take a look now, doctor," she says and leads me to a bed in the far end of the ward. There is a girl there who can't be more than eighteen. I see that she is breathing well, that she hasn't had a tracheostomy, that her drips are only Valium and saline solution. I look at her charts. Her temperature is scarcely above normal; her pulse and pressure only slightly high. She's just a little scared. The Valium will help. The Brigit doctor spins the curtain all the way around the bed, so that the three of us are inside a small tent. The doctor pulls down the bedcovers and lifts the girl's gown so we have a perfectly clear view of her trunk.

Perfectly clear: from just below her breasts to her pubic bone, her skin is as transparent as glass. I can see every throbbing organ, functioning flawlessly without apparent effort. Her lungs are a fresh light red; clearly she's never smoked. Her heart is small but pumping strongly, pure scarlet. Her brownish liver is as smooth as a baby's bottom, her ovaries are clean and feathery. I've never seen a healthier body.

"Skin grafts," says the doctor. "We've got to cover her up."

I think, *Cover up such beauty? Why? Why?* I touch her transparent skin; it has the exact texture a young girl's skin should have—strokable and warm and smooth. Why?

"She wants a life," the Brigit doctor whispers in my ear. "She wants to have lovers, to get married. What man could bear to see all this?"

I could, I'm thinking. I can't take my eyes away from her pulsing heart, from the delicacy of her ovaries, the rise and fall of her young lungs, the flow of clean red blood in her veins. I feel I have never beheld anything so perfect in my life.

"I'm afraid to undress except in the dark since this happened," the girl says. "I feel terrified that somehow there'll be a rip sometime and everything will fall out."

"Don't worry, that's no more likely to happen to you than to someone with ordinary skin. Do you know you're beautiful?"

"I know I'm a freak," she says.

So I look and look at her pancreas, her lovely liver, the wonderful length of her intestines. But my eyes are always drawn back to her heart and lungs. I am seeing life for the first time as it is lived on its basic level, before we begin to interfere with our minds, our cold steel instruments. I'm seeing the perfection of life. I stand there looking for hours, for days.

"HEY, NUALALA," I hear Brigit saying. "He's back." I open my eyes and see Nuala's huge green ones inches away. I blink rapidly, and tears form that I don't want. I am frustrated almost to death with my inability to communicate.

"You were gone for a while, buster," Brigit says. "It's about time you woke up. Don't scare us like that again."

Suddenly I'm aware of a burning pain low in my right chest.

The steel tube is gone, replaced by a curving length of plastic tubing coming out from between two ribs and disappearing over the edge of the bed. I think of the girl's perfect organs. I try to sit up, but I can't raise more than my head, and even that motion starts a stabbing pain where the tubing enters me. It must show on my face.

"Don't even think of asking for any more painkillers," Brigit says, smiling at me and wiping my face with a clean damp cloth. "Any more would kill a horse. You're at the max. If I were you, I'd be floating three feet off the bed, completely ecstatic."

I look at Nuala, hoping for a smile. But her straight heavy eyebrows are bent in a frown. She's done her hair differently today. I try to raise my hand to my head.

"You've got a headache? Impossible," says Brigit.

I wiggle my fingers in my hair.

"Oh, Nualala's new do? You like her new haircut? Good. She had it done just for you," Brigit says.

"Ah, Brigit, you're a tit," Nuala says. "Always the chatter."

For a moment in my dazed state, I think it's almost possible that Nuala may have done a thing like that. Then of course I realize that Nuala lives in a different world; we only intersect at a specific place at specific times. I have not yet made a world for her. And then it occurs to me that my motives aren't as pure as I thought. I want to make a world for Nuala where I'd be welcomed too, and that's not fair. That's a gift with a condition. That's not what I want. I want her to have what will make her happy, whether it has anything to do with me or not. The idea of me in

Nuala's world should never enter my mind. I used to have more control of my mind; I had a strong will and strict standards. But it seems that as my body deteriorates my mind does too. I wonder, if I survive this, will I have the mind I used to, the one I thought I knew?

I think I have been enough to the brink so that I've come to terms with death. And I believe I could handle some disabilities, difficulty walking, maybe even a wheelchair—if I survive. But right now I can't read; I haven't the attention and the words don't make much sense. My thoughts too seem to wander; they seem fuzzy, I can't follow one point to another in the usual way of logic. I don't want to survive an idiot, or even just dull. I would rather have my plug pulled if that is the way it's going to be. But who will know? And who will understand when in my silent way I beg to be disconnected from the life support that keeps me going now? I don't think I could invent a worse nightmare.

I'd like to tell Nuala about the girl in the hospital with the transparent skin. I think she would understand the beauty of it, and why I stood staring at her for days and days.

Instead I do something very stupid.

MY FRIEND CLARE comes to visit, carrying with her a board that has the letters of the alphabet written large on it. She writes down the letters I point to. It's tedious and upsetting because there are words I seem to forget the spelling of in the middle of trying. But one evening I get a message through: GET NUALA A PUPPY FOR ME. Clare thinks it's a great idea; she's always liking to give presents but doesn't always think about appropriateness.

Clare found me years ago in the Bells of Hell, shortly after I'd been badly rocked by a woman I loved. The woman knew she didn't have to play so rough but did it anyway, for reasons I've pondered ever since. Clare liked to have protégés, the more troubled the better. It was her mission to save us. She had two lives, really: a normal one with lovers and long-term relationships, and her secret one, collecting lost souls. She had more than enough vitality for both, and she could charm her way into and out of any situation she chose, uptown or downtown. She moved through the city without friction, slick as an eel.

I suppose I got the usual course of treatment. For a while we simply had drinks or dinner or saw a play together. Then she began inviting other friends to join us. And when two of those friends clicked, she was delighted. Over the course of a year I had affairs with an Indonesian artist she knew, an eighteen-year-old model Clare felt would benefit from having an older lover, and a television producer. All that put me back together, and although I graduated from protégé to friend, we stayed very close, seeing each other at least a couple of evenings a week.

People often misunderstood Clare's interest in them. They were suspicious, in that New York way, of anyone who seemed to give without any thought of being paid back. Even now she was my best friend; she lied her way into the ICU by claiming to be my half sister and my nearest living relative. She was implacable, and the hospital administration caved in before her assault. It was Clare who brought me to the hospital. She dropped by my loft one afternoon and found me hallucinating with fever.

THE FIRST FEW TIMES Clare had come to the ICU, she saw me fever-dark and swollen, my hair unwashed and face unshaven. She also saw how the staff was treating me: another job, another body. Work on it; fix it or not; move it on. They were not, to Clare's mind, seeing me as a man with loves and friends, a home and a job, a sense of humor and of honor—everything that makes up a life.

So she brought in a color snapshot from a skiing vacation. It just showed my face, happy and exhilarated. She taped it up above my bed.

"That's him?" everyone asked when they first saw it. "Yes," Clare would say emphatically. "Yes."

Suddenly I became a person to the doctors and nurses, not just a broken body. Now they could at least imagine I'd been someone like them.

Although Clare's clever tactic was opaque to me at first, I noticed the change very soon. Everyone was friendlier. That's when I really began to know Nuala and Brigit. Brigit first. She couldn't restrain her spirits and her chatter and, when she wasn't chaffing me, took the trouble to explain all my IVs and what painkillers I was being given and why I had a tube down my throat. I'd coughed up about a pint of bloody phlegm, and the oxygen levels in my blood were dangerously low. It turns out that if they get low enough, you slip into a coma. And unless they can raise the oxygen, you die.

It's supposed to be the most pleasant way to die. Pneumonia, the old man's friend.

I slipped into a coma after about two weeks, and that's when they gave me the tracheostomy. From then on, my life belonged to The Machine. I was one of its creatures, alive as long as I remained connected, as long as I obeyed it.

Soon I was closer to death than life. They upped the antibiotics as high as they dared, they punched drainage holes in my chest to drain the pus and mucus, and for a while I ceased to exist on the same plane as everyone else who came and went in my room.

I doubt this turn made any difference to Brigit and Nuala. They'd seen worse and wouldn't be surprised to walk into my room one morning and find a corpse. They'd get a crew to remove the corpse, but they'd keep the photo for Clare. They weren't sure what Clare and I were to each other, but it didn't matter. She was the person who came to see me. They'd say they were sorry, as they had so many times to so many people, when Clare came that day and saw only an empty bed.

But Clare was there every evening. She badgered every doctor she saw about my treatment; she argued relentlessly that they should try new drugs when one bacterial pneumonia was defeated, only to be superceded by another kind. She raged that they should be more exact about the pressure The Machine exerted on my lungs, and the rate at which it inflated them.

Clare became the terror of the ICU.

But I think the relentless assaults of pneumonia were also the beginning of her great fear.

SO NOW, CRISIS PASSED, Clare goes to the pound and finds a very young part-Lab, part-shepherd female whose aggressive affection is amazing. She smuggles it into my ward one afternoon in a box, and when Nuala comes around, smiling for a change, I point to the box with the red ribbon.

"It's for you. He asked for it for you," Clare tells her. The smile goes away. She looks perturbed. "Unwrap it," Clare says. Nuala does, and the mutt falls all over herself trying to scramble into Nuala's arms, her long pink tongue lapping at Nuala's face. Clare's laughing, Brigit runs over and wants to pet the little thing at once, but Nuala just stands there holding her in that same awkward way men hold babies. She puts her back in the box and asks Clare to step outside the ward.

Clare comes back alone, looking defeated. "Nuala doesn't want a dog. She doesn't have time to take care of one. She's taking it back to the pound tomorrow. Cold bitch."

"That's just like Nuala," Brigit says. "She's probably afraid she'll get too attached to the dog and it'll disrupt her life. As if there was anything to disrupt. As if she didn't have plenty of room in her life. Jesus, a puppy."

5

NUALA WASN'T ON DUTY for four full days. I
wallowed in my misery.

Try to lie in one position for four days. Watch
the nurses and doctors come and go, healthy, able not
only to walk but to bend and stretch and reach and
tell each other jokes and say a few cheerful words to
a patient. Imagine them leaving the ward when their
work is done, having dinner in a Thai restaurant, going to a movie. Imagine them seeing some friends for
drinks, picking up their dry cleaning, going for a walk
through Washington Square Park late in the day when
the sun is soft and golden. Brigit is doing these things
too, no doubt. But it's also likely she's had decent, if
not extraordinary, sex in her own bed with a man she
desires on at least one of those nights, and may have

lain lazily nude in bed the next morning, arms thrown back, round breasts rising, until the man realized his luck and did it to her again.

I don't think Nuala's that lucky. She'll meet Brigit for drinks at the Bells some nights, but people say she's very possessive of her time off. She likes to go her own way, alone. She'll happily spend an entire day in just one section of the Metropolitan Museum, or breeze through the Frick and the Whitney both. In all sorts of weather, she'll ride the ferry back and forth between Battery Park and Staten Island half a dozen times or more, just for the pleasure of being on the water. She can browse in art supply houses like Canal Paints or Utrecht for hours, ideas filling her head, but she never buys a thing. She likes hardware stores too. And shooting pool. In the afternoons she likes to go to a little English place not far from the hospital and have Devonshire tea. Sometimes when her mood is right, she'll take herself to a sexy R-rated movie—the early show.

Maybe that's what Nuala was doing today, alone in a theater on a sunny Sunday afternoon, crisp spring weather by the look and motion of the clouds. I'd almost forgotten what it was like to lie with someone, skin to skin. If I couldn't, I wished at least I could sit next to Nuala and see it. I needed some escape. I wished I could read and tried but gave up after a paragraph. It was a heavy hardback and I couldn't hold it upright for very long, and I had to read the first paragraph three times before I had even a vague idea what it said.

A blood lady came to take some and couldn't find any veins on my arm, so she took from between my left big toe and the next. The blood ladies came every couple of days, carrying their red cases that looked like shoe-shine kits. They were all Japanese, just like the aides who washed and shaved us and made our beds were all Jamaican. One Jamaican woman, the one who'd appeared as a nurse in my last coma, liked me. She'd come over for no reason, grip my hand in hers, and put her round black face very close to mine. "You doin' good, man, you lookin' fresh today," she'd say, grinning the broadest grin.

But on this Sunday, nobody came near me after the blood lady. I had some friends who might have liked to come, my partner might have wanted to see me, but no one but Clare was able to get around the rule that only family members could enter the ICU rooms. One or two other patients had visitors. The patient next to me was Hispanic, and her three daughters were all there. They shrieked at each other in high, rapid, rough Caribbean Spanish. I hated the sound of it. I liked the soft lisping Castillian of a girl I once went out with.

I could just reach the TV controls. I turned it on. Only two channels seemed to be working: one with a movie about a woman dying of cancer, which upset her husband, played by Anthony Hopkins, very much, and one with a golf match. I felt more drugged than usual, watching the unfamiliar rituals of golf, and the players' remarkably similar ways of walking, looking, and swinging, hearing the soft voices of the announcers, the soft polite applause of the crowd. It was impossible to figure out who was winning. It was difficult to know even what the point of the walking and swinging was, until I heard the prize money mentioned: about six years of my pay. I wondered if my drug dosage had been mistakenly altered, but I had no way to ask. All I could do was blearily stare at the endless green of the golf course (which was like some beautiful eighteenth-century English landscape) and outside at the endless blowing horsetail clouds.

The day was very slow. I couldn't even seem to nap.

And yet that night I couldn't sleep. I rang for the nurse, hoping she could read my lips if I asked for more drugs. Nobody came for a long time. When somebody did, she understood what I was asking for but said I had already been given the dose the doctor authorized. She couldn't give me more. They were all very rigid like that; you never could convince a nurse to give you more than the doctor had written down, even if the handwriting was so bad the number of milligrams was highly debatable.

There was a bright half-moon that night and for a while I watched thin clouds race past it. I felt like I was losing my moorings, like my mind was leaving me, going off someplace by itself. I concentrated on the moon, and tried to remember that poem everyone learns in elementary school: The moon was a ghostly galleon, tossed upon stormy seas/the road was a river of moonlight—a blank here—And the highwayman came riding, riding . . . It wasn't an Irish poem I don't think, but it made me think of Ireland anyway. I've never been there. I'm sure my imagination is a generation or two out of date. Or it may have come completely out of books and movies, every Irish girl looking like Maureen O'Hara in *The Quiet Man*, every village so peaceful a mix of Catholics and Protestants.

In the world I'd make for Nuala, she'd live in Ireland, I think, in a lovely little cottage with roses along the walk and geraniums in

the windowpots. The cottage would be whitewashed inside and out,
with ancient beams of wood so dark they were almost black. The
front door would be painted a deep, rich red. Nuala's man would
be up first, out feeding the Connemara pony that pulled their gig,
and forking hay to the cattle. Nuala would still be in bed, stretching
her limbs luxuriously under linen sheets. She'd think a little about
New York and the one bad thing that happened, and she'd be glad
to be in a place so safe.

She'd get up and make strong tea, oatmeal with fresh cream,
and toast. She'd eat with her man and smile at him across the
little kitchen table that had belonged to her great-grandmother.
She'd be wearing a cream cable-knit sweater and corduroy trousers tucked into Wellingtons. Her hair would be loose and wild
as the gorse that sprawled all over the ridge behind the cottage.

She's going to get pregnant one of these days soon.

It's a picture postcard sort of world, the stupidest illusion you
can have. Anyone who's ever traveled anyplace knows that for sure.
Yet that's the best my mind can come up with just now. Maybe
some depth and texture will come another time, and some sense of
reality.

Nuala will require this, I know. She won't live in dream-
time.

BRIGIT WAKES ME UP the next morning by tickling my nose with
a cotton swab. When I open my eyes I see her grinning her gap-

toothed grin. I see Nuala's back in the room across from mine. Brigit puts her face close to mine, looking at the IV in my neck, the most treacherous one, the potential killer. "She kept the damn dog, buster!" she whispers. "She's named it Sinead and walks it in the park every evening. She even lets it sleep at the foot of her bed."

I nod. But I won't smile today; it seems too futile.

"You might have been a decent boyfriend to have before you got hit with all this," she says.

I nod. My spastic left hand, the one with the bent wrist and the hand closed like a claw, chooses this moment to fall off the bed rail and land near my groin.

"Not yet!" she says, laughing. "When you're better. And when I find out whatever it is you've got going with that Clare. Is she English? Is her hair always that color?"

"Brigit," Nuala calls. "When you're finished your morning gossip, can you come over here and give me a hand with Mrs. Petacci? We've got to suction."

Ah, God, I hated that. Every few hours they'd disconnect the blue tube from the valve sewn into the hole in your throat and stick a little vacuum cleaner inside. It made you cough and gag until you thought you'd asphyxiate, sucking out all this thick slimy green mucus that accumulated in your trachea. Only one thing made it bearable: the clean crisp breaths you could take once they put the blue tubing back. Really for a while it felt like being on top of the Alps, inhaling the most beautiful clean air in the world.

Later that day Nuala did the job on me. It took two for Mrs. Petacci because her neck was so fat that one person had to hold folds of skin out of the way while the other suctioned. I didn't like it much when it was Nuala who got the dirty jobs on me, but it never seemed to matter to her whether it was the suction or the catheter. And I knew it was grosser when I checked out; it was worse than cleaning up after a baby.

I began to believe the body was just another Machine that manufactured mucus and other sordid things twenty-four hours a day, every day, though there was no use for any of them.

I preferred not to think of what it might be like in my room when I was checked out. I knew that I was unresponsive to any stimulus at all, scarcely human except to those like Brigit who believed the subconscious was still in touch with the world. Yet I was embarrassed about what she and Nuala would see my slab-of-meat body doing, left to its own natural devices. If I'd had enough blood pressure, I'd have blushed contemplating it.

THAT EVENING Clare comes in with a pair of bright purple Chuck Taylor high-tops. She puts them on my feet. "Have to do it," she says, stringing the laces. "Nuala says you've been lying here so long you're getting foot drop. It means your ligaments are stretching. It's like being a ballet dancer en pointe for hours and hours. You'll be crippled unless we get your feet in an L-position. It can take surgery to correct bad foot drop."

So there I lay, thin as a camp inmate, my bones making sharp outlines under the sheet, with a giant pair of purple Chuck Taylors sticking out at the end of the bed for all to see. All do see, and everyone feels compelled to say a few words. My Jamaican with the perfect round face grins like a maniac. She wears a little tropical scent you can smell when she leans close, which she likes to do. She must be fearless; she doesn't care what germs you're loaded with. "Righteous shoes, man. You be playing hoops before you know it. That purple's sharp. Raises the tone of the ward."

"Pretty close to the color of her hair, aren't they?" wicked Brigit says when Clare's left the ward to hunt down whatever doctors happen to be on the floor. She's sure tonight from the way I'm breathing that The Machine is going too fast for me. She drags a doctor in, he observes for a few minutes, then actually slows down the pumping a little bit. Brigit's making faces behind their backs. Brigit doesn't much like the way Clare can persuade doctors to listen to her; the doctors tend to treat the nurses as inferior, even if they value their specific skills, which can be formidable. Most of the nurses are smoother and gentler in handling problems with my IVs and the trache than the doctors are.

I make no sign to Nuala about Sinead the mutt. And Nuala never says a word to me about it. She is neither more nor less friendly or attentive. I find this pleasing. It feels like a proper balance. I would hate it if she seemed obliged to me. We just communicate in our awkward, halting way about the daily medical necessities. But I don't check out for over a week.

It's exciting to think that Nuala's silence is a signal she suspects my secret world-making business. I begin to believe Brigit can be one of my agents, like Clare. I can't use the alphabet board with Brigit—it would be too obvious—but I begin to feel we have a link, that maybe I can put thoughts in Brigit's mind just by staring at her. She always stares back, as if she's slightly mesmerized, which I take to mean she is reading me, as women sometimes can.

Before I got sick, I thought this sort of thing was the worst sort of bullshit. Now, because of where I've been and what I've seen, I'm not quite so cynical.

And Clare has given me a great gift, one I may use when the time seems right: her alphabet board.

6

THE FIRST TIME MYALA BHUTO SWIRLED into my room, I thought I was hallucinating and mouthed, Go away, go away.

"Oh, we are not here for going but for breathing therapy!" she replied happily, wagging her head slightly from side to side.

I didn't believe in her.

Myala was one of those tall, striking Pakistani girls with skin the beautiful shade of creamy coffee. She had a thin hawk's nose with a diamond stud in one nostril, a red dot in the middle of her forehead, and enough gold bangles to outfit a gypsy band. And she had a miraculous way of wearing her white uniform as if it were a silk sari, carrying it at an angle across her narrow hips so that it looked as if she were swaying and dancing when she walked. "Just one jiffy, we are making the therapy," she said, displaying the most perfect white teeth I had ever seen.

She opened the black bag she was carrying and took out a bottle of what looked liked crushed herbs. She placed them in a blue plastic globe with a valve on one side. Then from another bottle she poured in some liquid that smelled bitter, and the concoction began to foam and smoke. Almost faster than I could see, her incredibly thin fingers plugged her blue globe into my blue tube, and I was breathing the bitter smoke. But there was no choking, no unpleasant sensation. It was soothing. "Yes, we are doing your poor ill lungs very good with this," Myala said, looking at me with her kohl-rimmed eyes. "Opening passages and so forth, reducing awful mucus."

The procedure was due to last about twelve minutes, she told me. She sat patiently by my bed, still a figure from a fever dream except for the calmness in her voice. She noticed the photo above my bed. I saw her study the photo, look at me, and then go back to studying the photo. "Very handsome, your snap. Soon you are looking just like that again, oh, yes," Myala said, showing me her brilliant teeth again in a broad smile. "Watch out, virgin girls!" she said, laughing. "Very good-looking."

When she'd left, I was still wondering whether my mind had made it all up. But then Nuala and Brigit came in, Brigit doing a short Irish imitation of Myala's tall Pakistani sway. "Ah, so Miss Marriage is thinking you are a very handsome fellow, by jove,"

Brigit said. "Watch out, all you virgin girls, pretty soon he is out prowling, my goodness."

"Miss Marriage may never let him leave the hospital if all that ugly crud on his face does go away," Nuala said. "She may keep him, to protect all the virgin Paki girls out there."

"Graceful neck, but legs thin as sticks, that type," Brigit said. "Miss Marriage casts her I-very-much-doubt virgin eye on every new resident. She isn't beneath having a go at suitable patients. Now you watch her hands when she's in here. Don't let her touch you anywhere you wouldn't let me."

"Oh, very handsome fellow," Nuala said. She seems unusually bright today. I'm thinking there must be some wonderful stories circulating about Miss Marriage. But I mouth, Bad girls. Just jealous.

"Women, not girls, to you. Remember, we're your nurses and you don't want to get on the wrong side of us," Brigit said. Nuala is switching one of my IV bags, pain or antibiotics I can't tell anymore. Brigit's got me out of the fog, though.

You virgin? I mouth to Brigit.

"Is the pope Catholic? What else would a fine colleen like meself be. I'm saving up for marriage."

I mouth, No loss.

Brigit picks up my urine bag. It's about three-quarters full. "Here, Nuala, just switch this with the fentanyl bag. This sod'll never know the difference, and we can have the fentanyl for ourselves."

I turn my head to see Nuala reaching up to hook the new anti-biotic bag. She's on her toes and stretching up her arms. I'm hoping to see her breasts, but there doesn't seem to be anything there. Brigit's the bouncy one, all over: breasts, ass, little belly.

I can still think like this, sick as I am, but I try not to, because there's never even the slightest stirring where there ought to be, and that worries me. I'm obsesssed with it, actually; I feel part of me never came out of the coma I fell into.

Still, late that night after my sleeping shots, I'm lying there thinking about Myala. I'm imagining an intertwining of limbs, her dark thin ones and my pale stronger ones. It's going great until I imagine her singsong: "Oh, yes, we are loving each other up just right, handsome fellow."

Myala's visits soon become like almost everything else in the hospital—except that first cold slice of a scalpel so sharp the cut doesn't even start to bleed for a minute—routine, and later, unnoticed.

7

I WAS HALF-ASLEEP one morning when Brigit came limping into my room with vast brown scabs on both knees. Nuala followed her in. I instantly closed my eyes again. Sometimes I could get away with this, and they'd talk freely whenever they thought I was out.

"I don't suppose you'll be going off from the Bells again at three in the morning with a guy you never met before on a Harley," I hear Nuala say.

"I'm seeing him tonight, if it's any of your business," Brigit says, sounding cross and tired.

"You're mad. You meet some tattooed biker, he buys you a few beers, and off you go, drunk. Jesus and Mary, girl."

"We weren't going that fast, and it wasn't really his fault. The rear wheel just spun out from under us on wet cobblestones on Perry Street. We crashed into a lot of trash cans. Nothing very dramatic."

"Brigit, you're an idiot."

"Wait a sec. He was so cool about it! He just left the bike lying there in all the garbage and walked me to his place. I sewed up the one bad cut he had on his forearm. He never flinched. And then—he actually licked the scrapes on my knees. Of course, it may have been the Ecstasy, but when he was doing it to me I fell in love with him."

"Jaysus. Bloody Jaysus," Nuala says, her accent thickening. "You bloody maniac. Why don't you just throw yourself in the river?"

"You think I have a death wish? Nuala! Look around here. Sooner or later, we're going to wind up in one of these beds ourselves. Christ, look at Blatchley here. Out of nowhere, a perfectly healthy man is nearly struck dead by little bugs we can't even detect. You can't deny it. You can't. I'm just making sure I live some life as well as I can before I wind up like this one here."

"Whose heart rate is increasing, which means the sneaky bastard is probably awake," Nuala says. Then she grabs the fleshy bit between my thumb and forefinger and pinches as hard as she can. My eyes pop wide open.

"If you ever repeat what you hear from us when you get well, we'll hunt you down and torture you with syringes. We know how to make them really hurt, better believe it," Nuala says. But there's a light in her eyes I like.

Great knees, I mouth to Brigit. Scabs fashion now?

"What? Ah, joke if you want. You're harmless. Who's he going to tell, anyway—that Clare? Some of his smarmy friends? It's not like they'll have our names and phone numbers."

"No," Nuala says, "but they could hang around the Bells, pretending to be bikers, since your taste would be known to run that way."

"No chance. I've got my biker," Brigit says.

For the first time I gesture for my alphabet board, which has been propped on the windowsill since the night Clare left it for me. Nuala writes the letters down.

ONLY WIMP CRASH A HARLEY INTO TRASH AND BLAME COBBLE-STONES.

"You wish you were a wimp like this guy," Brigit snapped.

BET I COULD DO BETTER. LOTS OF EXPERIENCE.

Brigit starts laughing.

"You are filthy-minded, Mr. Blatchley," Nuala says. But she's laughing too.

THAT NIGHT I HAD A LATE NIGHTMARE, the kind that wakes you to a ruined dawn and sometimes spoils the entire day. I was trying to suction myself, in the dream, and the mucus wouldn't stop flowing. I filled one tube, threw it away, filled another, threw that away, filled a third and a fourth and a fifth. The floor around my bed was covered with suction tubes crammed with the green sticky gunk your lungs produce. I had to hurry, because I was losing consciousness and needed to hook myself back up to The Machine.

The Machine was whispering, "You are pulling your own plug. You are about to become a suicide," in its wet, bubbling voice that I so detested and that haunted my nights. Nuala was standing in the doorway. She was saying not to do it that way. "If you want to go, I'll help you. Brigit and I will help. We'll make it look natural. They won't even be able to tell in the autopsy. They'll say the bacteria finally won."

"Or," Brigit said, sweeping up the tubes of mucus, "we'll bring you a bottle of Bushmills. You can drink it after a morphine shot and you'll never know you died."

"He can't drink. The hole in his throat," Nuala said.

"Then we'll put it in his feed bag. Better that way, anyway, in case he doesn't like Irish whiskey."

"Like me," Nuala said.

"Don't worry," Brigit said. "We'll find a way to check you out. When you're really ready, just say so. We'll take care of you. We won't let you suffer."

My feet are cold, so cold, I mouthed. Nuala piled a folded blanket over them. Then I felt a strange wet warmth all over the right side of my chest. I woke up. A stitch had torn in the incision they'd made for a new drainage tube.

"The clogged lung is a toilet, and I'm the plumber. You should see my hourly rate," the pulmonary specialist said, assuming I couldn't hear.

There was a scarlet puddle on the bed, and a spreading light-red nimbus. Blood, fresh blood, was a beautiful dark thick color.

I wondered why painters hadn't used it more often. I watched my puddle thickening and growing.

I thought, *No one here knows my name. No one here will remember my name. They'll think, "Oh, he was the one with that crazy friend Clare, the one who swore he was never a drug user despite his high tolerances. The one who wasn't HIV-positive but whose body acted like it was. Poor fuck. Too bad."*

My favorite night nurse, Susan, came in then for a last check before the shift turned over. She saw the puddle of blood. "Goddamn surgeons couldn't darn a sock," she muttered. She came back with pressure bandages and a package with a threaded needle. She wiped down my side, saw where the blood was leaking, and made two neat stitches. Then she watched for a while to see if there was any more bleeding. There wasn't. "I think I'll leave the mess, a little mystery for Nuala and Brigit," she said. Susan had blond hair and was from Baltimore. She told me that one night when I was sleepless. It turned out her father and I had gone to the same high school, and not that far apart, either, which made me feel old, since she was already twenty-three. She seemed so bright she probably should have been in med school herself rather than nursing in an ICU. But people do what they want, don't they?

Nuala and Brigit were too seasoned for Susan, though. When they arrived thirty minutes later, they didn't blink at the congealing puddle of blood. They could see I wasn't leaking from where the tube entered, and they saw the two fresh stitches. "Susan the surgeon," Nuala said. She sounded contemptuous. They pretended it wasn't even blood.

"So we've got a bed wetter. I'm disgusted. At your age. Let me just check your catheter," Nuala said.

"No, that's my job, you're the virgin," Brigit said, pulling down my covers and taking my cold, shy penis in her hand. "No problems here."

Then they hurt me. They lifted me up to a sitting position, swung my wasted legs over the edge of the bed, and lifted me into a wheelchair. I bit my lip hard against the pain. They stripped off my blood-soaked gown. My reflex was to huddle, though they'd seen me naked a dozen times before. They at least had the grace to tie me into a fresh gown before they tore away the bloody sheets and remade my bed. My head felt very loosely attached to my neck. It wanted to loll. The pressure of the chair on my emaciated ass was killing me. God, how I wished they'd hurry. I could taste blood on my lip.

"Not tough enough for the chair?" Brigit said. "You wuss. We'll tuck you back in, and you can spend the whole rest of the day just lying there like an old man."

The hurt was worse when they lifted me from the chair and laid me on the bed. I was breathing too fast; I felt close to collapse. And I felt anger. Why had they been so rough? I gestured weakly for my alphabet board. Nuala handed it to me.

BAD FUCK LAST NIGHT, BRIGIT?

"That'd be none of your bloody business," she said.

PMS?

"No, smartass. I woke up alone, and on the wrong side of my chilly old bed."

SO TAKE OUT ON ME?

"You're here, aren't you? You're available. You want me to take it out on poor little old Mrs. Petacci, give her a cerebral hemorrhage?"

Nuala gives me relief; she turns on the fentanyl drip. I think Brigit must have missed hers. She's never this crabby when her little baby needle has done its job.

"You've got an easy day today," Nuala said. "Nothing to do until Cindy comes after lunch. You can just take it easy and enjoy your drips. How's that milk shake taste this morning?"

YUM

AS THE PAIN FADES, I'm wondering how Nuala spent her night. I have my ideas. I also have my ideas of how I wished it was: She'd have a good man who looked after her. She'd have woken on the right side of the bed this morning, and he'd already be up. He'd have brewed some good coffee and heated a couple of muffins. I make great coffee. I'd smile at her across the kitchen table where we'd be sitting, still in our robes. Later, as she left, I'd wrap her in my arms and give her a kiss deep enough to last all day and send her off with a smile on her face.

I don't think she has that pleasant a situation at the moment.

The smile's missing too many mornings. And surely it wouldn't be me she'd have in mind.

I wonder if Nuala's da liked her more than her mother did. Or was it the opposite? It's never even, is it? It unbalances you in your life later on, being favored by one parent more than the other. It affects the way you deal with men and women. Either way, it's something that has to be overcome.

I'm a fucking idiot, of course. A man in my position who allows himself to become emotionally dependent on a woman who is taking care of him is more than just stupid. He's demented. He needs a shrink.

Or I should just keep my fantasies in check for a while, since I'm useless anyhow. I could just ride out this entire experience and leave without a single pang for an Irish girl with wild hair and thick straight eyebrows.

I should be thinking only about getting better. I should be doing New Age things like visualizing healthy lungs, a brain that makes all its synapses, a body that doesn't run up a temperature of 103 every time a new bug pays a call.

But I am so alone my heart feels cracked.

THE RESIDENT NUN COMES BY every other day and puts holy water on my left wrist and then makes a cross with it on my forehead. She says it comes from a holy shrine of miracles in Mexico. I don't feel too confident about it and suggest she save it for the more gravely ill. She says I shouldn't worry—she goes there every year and gets jugs of the stuff.

CLARE HAS brought me one of those wonderfully photographed Time-Life books on the body. I can't manage an attention span of more than a few minutes, but I like to look at the photos of lungs. They're very pinkish and delicate-looking, pods of life filled inside with tiny flowers, thousands of them, where the atom of oxygen actually joins with a cell of blood. The concept is majestic, that something as large as a human body should depend absolutely on the miraculous processes at the levels of molecules and single cells. I would love to see the exact moment an oxygen atom enters a red blood cell. That's my problem. The oxygen can't get through the pus and cellular debris that are clogging and ruining my tiny flowers. The bacteria are attacking the flowers and rotting them, leaving scar tissue behind and toxic wastes that flow off to pollute the rest of my system. It's a race really to see if the doctors can come up with some combination of antibiotics that will kill the bacteria before the bacteria kill the flowers and corrupt my blood beyond redemption.

This is not very positive thinking. This is doing me no good.

I would like once to sit and have a civilized conversation with Nuala about life. I sense that I have things to learn from her, even though from what little I know of her life her experience hasn't been nearly as broad as mine. But there's perspective, alertness, and extrapolation. Maybe she's better at those things than I am. Or maybe she's just overly serious, with little sense of humor and nothing at all to say about how life might best be lived.

I wish there was some electrical device they could hook up to my blue tube so I could speak. They have them for people who have lost their larynx to cancer. They make a croaking sort of sound, but you can understand them.

Cindy, the physical therapist, arrives just at that time of day when the sinking sun is reflecting directly into my room from a tall glass building a few blocks away. She is grinning, dressed as usual as if she's going to the gym, and carrying two black boxes that look like very elaborate, professional Walkmen.

"Hey," she says. "You're going to learn about Edison to-day."

She plugs one of the Walkmen into a socket in the wall. She takes a tube of grease and puts a few dabs on my frozen left hand and wrist. Then she attaches electrodes from the second Walkman over the grease spots. I'm not liking the look of this, and I like it even less when she cables the two Walkmen together and I can feel a strong electrical buzzing in my hand and wrist; it's like touching a badly connected light switch.

"Now we'll see if you've got some usable nerves in that claw or not," Cindy says, ratcheting up a dial. I feel like I've stuck a key into an electric socket. Everything tingles just below the point of unbearable pain, and my wrist snaps straight. She ratchets down the juice and my wrist collapses. She powers up, and it jumps straight again. "Cool," Cindy says. "You're not hopeless at all. We just have to keep it working." So for ten minutes she shoots voltage into me and laughs each time my wrist goes rigidly straight.

I feel like a frog in a high school science experiment. Cindy looks like she thinks she's going to get an A.

8

IF NUALA HAS ELEVEN KINDS OF RAIN and mist where she comes from, I've got at least as many types of days. It takes experience to recognize this. On the surface, tissue-thin as it is, every day's the same: the routines, the light in the room, the delicate pressure of the sheets on my body, the stinging of the IVs, the ache in the small of my back because I can't move much.

Yet there are so many days with odd, unpredictable tones. Sometimes I feel hyperalert, sometimes dull. Sometimes everything is hazy, as if I can't quite wake up entirely. Sometimes I have no idea at first where I am or how I got there. Sometimes I feel glad to be there, because I have no responsibility at all; nothing is expected of me.

The nurses are sensitive to these different days. They each have their methods and their styles. When I'm alert they like to joke and banter, to keep it all so light that even I become lighthearted. Brigit's tactic to break through a fog is talking to me as if I'm perfectly lucid. Nuala behaves as if I'm out of it and can't understand exactly what's going on. She doesn't want to force her way through. She treats me as if my mind is somewhere else. She's challenging me to bring myself back. It seems to relax her somehow.

What happens when the two of them are together is that Nuala usually wins. They talk to each other as if I'm asleep, or comatose. That's how I learned Brigit had gotten chlamydia from her biker and ditched him. That's how I learned Nuala was getting worse cramps with every period and was worried she might have a cyst. That's how I heard which night nurse is having an affair with a third-year resident, who unfortunately has caught TB from some patient and is on a strict drug regime.

THEY CAME INTO MY ROOM around lunchtime on one of the foggy days, wearing their coats over their uniforms. "How's your milk shake?" Brigit asks. I'm confused, until I remember that at the back of my throat there is almost always the taste of vanilla from the high-protein liquid they're pumping into me.

"Are you in a bank, an airport, or a hotel?" Nuala says.

I think that I mouth, Hotel. But I can't be sure I've actually done it.

"He's drugged up to the eyes. They change his mix on the night shift?" Nuala asks Brigit.

"Well, while you're lying here in the sun enjoying your milk shake, we're spending our lunch hour going down to Eighth Street to buy shoes," Brigit says. "We need new shoes."

This sounds serious. I nod and mouth: New shoes.

Brigit laughs, but Nuala looks at her as if she's doing something mean.

"Give it a rest, will you? He doesn't know what you're talking about," Nuala says, and they leave.

No one looks in on me for a while. I start to fiddle with the IVs and manage to detach one. It must be the fentanyl, because pretty soon I'm feeling really restless. If it didn't hurt so much to move, I'd try to climb out of bed. I try to lie very still but it feels like I have spiders creeping around under my skin. I try counting my fingers, but by the time I get to six or seven I've forgotten where I started. I want to hear poems in my head, but of the dozen or so I've memorized I can only recall a few disjointed lines: I grow old, I grow old, I shall wear the bottoms of my trousers rolled and walk along the beach. But no mermaids will sing to me. Who said they exist, except sea-crazed sailors? I try to imagine if her smooth human skin above her scaly waist would taste fishy if you licked it. I would like to taste her salty lips; I would like to kiss her because she's from the sea, where life starts. Maybe I could live underwater with her. I wouldn't need The Machine; oxygen would come from the water that would fill my lungs. Suddenly I feel like I'm drowning. I try to scream for help, but no sound comes; the blue tube to The Machine stops the air before it can reach my vocal cords.

I'm never deaf, but I'm always mute.

The tube in my nose is soft and rubbery and clear. You can see what's flowing through it, if you pull enough out. I gently slide it out, slowly, inch by inch; it takes a long time because the tube must be three feet long, full of a thick white substance, exactly like a milk shake. Then I'm caught. Susan, who's usually on night duty, looks in on me. Although she's cross, she can't help laughing.

"This is not one of your better days," she says, reattaching the fentanyl drip. She and another one of the bad girls tie my wrists to the bed bars with white strips of cloth. Then she gives me a big needle of something in the shoulder and almost instantly I'm back where I started. In the fog I can barely move my arms; my legs are warm and painless. She leaves for a moment, or maybe an hour, and comes back with a resident, who threads the feeding tube back down my nose into my stomach. It's a bit tricky; you don't want the tube to go down the trachea and into the lungs. You'd drown in vanilla milk shake. For a while I'm perfectly conscious of this foreign body intruding so deeply in mine. I feel invaded. But it's not so awful this time. The fentanyl keeps making things easier and easier.

I'M DROWSY AND FLOATING when Nuala and Brigit come back into my room, still wearing their coats and carrying red and pink and black and yellow plastic bags, each one displaying the sharp corners of a rectangular box.

"Shoes!" Brigit says.

"Oh, he's still out of it," Nuala says.

"Seeing the colors will help," Brigit insists. "It's the same as when you hum songs to Mrs. Petacci."

She begins opening her boxes.

"I don't do that," Nuala says.

"I've heard those Irish lullabies. You think there's a chance they register something, even if it's just the presence of another human. It's a kindness, Nuala, not something to hide. I think buster here is never really out of it. Look at his eyes. Even when he's doped, he sees, Nuala. He sees you and recognizes you."

"Why me?"

"Something going on between you two I should know about?"

"Oh, get out, Brigit."

I'm sure I'm hearing all this. I think there are certain un-impeded passages, that this is registering in my brain somewhere where the drugs and the bugs don't reach. There's a core of my-self I can feel, a hidden center of my identity that won't be sedated or confused or overcome. But I have no benchmark. I have been drugged so long that I have no way to compare this with the way I was before. I can't control this center, maybe it's something new, an adaptation. It rules itself. Now it wants to shout at Nuala, "I know you! I see you have shoes!" But nothing comes out, just some gasps from my blue tube. They see the effort on my face, though.

"He's trying, look at him. He's trying," Brigit says. She puts a pair of bright yellow patent leather shoes with huge thick heels on the end of my bed. Then she sets up some beautiful brown suede boots with stilletto heels that must be six inches high. Finally she places a pair of electric blue Mary Janes in the row. She comes up to the head of the bed, to admire them from my perspective. I somehow make an OK gesture with my right hand. Brigit looks pleased. She pats my head. "Every pair sixty percent off, too," she says. "Come on, Nuala, show us what you got."

Nuala makes a face, but she unpacks a pair of motorcycle boots—the genuine article—the sort of thing you could wear on a Harley and feel well dressed. I believe Brigit must have influenced that purchase. Then she unwraps the most delicate little flats, Italian, obviously, a low slanted heel and a long low toe, in a walnut-brown lizard. They are so graceful. I can see her wearing them with thick Wolford stockings and a brown suede skirt about five inches above the knee. She'd look stunning and innocent, the way Italian high school girls can look. I've been to Italy a few times, and I have my impressions.

I smile and point to my alphabet board. Brigit hands it to me. VERY ELAJENT, SEXEY, SORRY, LETTERS COMIING FUNNNY TDAY. GREET SHOES. WOMAN SHOES SMELL SO GUD.

Nuala's already putting her new things away, but Brigit wants to admire hers awhile longer. "We've got to get back on duty," Nuala says.

Brigit asks me, "Can I leave these out for a while, so I can look at them when I come back?"

Of course I nod yes. I'm crazy about Brigit's attitude.

I'm really floating now, warm all over, better than I almost ever feel. The wet whistling of The Machine doesn't even get me down. I have a samba CD Clare brought me. I point, and Brigit puts it on. Inside my rigid body I am moving, swaying to the samba rhythms. I forget about myself for a while. I wander paths in my memory that have been blocked. I remember the first time I sat on the top of the Alps. I climbed and watched the sun going down behind the ranges that ran all the way to the cloudless horizon, and I thought for a moment that I believed in God. Nothing so perfect could be random. Then I almost broke my ankle coming down in the deepening dusk. And I remember a beautiful Swiss girl with a baby in her lap, sitting ten feet away from me on a park bench on the shore of Lake Lugano. We stared at each other for at least twenty minutes and never said a word. She looked back once as she walked away, her page boy hair swinging. The connection that is meant to be made but never is because we are all at heart afraid of each other.

I'M ADMIRING BRIGIT'S SHOES at the end of my bed. The colors look brighter now. I'm seeing the smooth skin of her feet slipping into them; I'm seeing her walk out of her apartment feeling especially spunky. I'm seeing her drinking at the Bells of Hell with some guy, maybe even going home with him, but the lout will be so eager for tits and ass that he'll never notice the perfect sexiness of her shoes. Girls must be resigned to that, I think. I know I made some fine connections when I was well by paying attention to shoes and scarves and bags and great haircuts. It gave my women a nice feeling that maybe I understood them a little.

I doze.

When I awake, Brigit's shoes are gone. But Nuala's there, sitting in a chair pulled close to my bed. She wipes my face with a damp cloth; she knows I love this. She says, "You're almost cool, I think. Try to stick around. There are things I want to tell you."

9

NIGHT BECOMES DAY for me before anyone else. Nuala makes that happen.

There's the softest light you can imagine, the translucent sort of light in watercolor paintings. I'm standing on a stone jetty, looking landward at a small congregation of houses and shops, some whitewashed with doors and windowsills in primary colors, others painted with pastel yellows and soft blues and thin red washes. At the far end is a small Gothic church of brown stone. Along the quay moves a line of those Irish carts with seats that run the length of either side. The carts are packed with girls. They are wearing First Communion dresses, lovely white dresses on which mothers have spared no expense even though they'll only be worn once; there's an abundance of fine lace, hand embroidery, and hand-beading at cuffs, hems, and necks. In the second cart I see Nuala. She waves to me. Her wild reddish hair has been gathered and braided close to her head. Her eyes look huge. The carts are drawn by glossy white ponies, and the people of the village march behind them toward the church. The bells are ringing wildly.

It's low tide. Boats of horizon blue, shimmering green, and lemony yellow rest in the mud alongside the jetty. You can smell that salty iodine odor of whelks and mussels and kelp.

Then I'm standing next to Nuala as she leaves the church. She's nothing but a happy schoolgirl, glowing cheeks, proud of her white dress. Not even a hint of breasts or hips, as straight as a boy.

"You've got it all wrong," she says to me before walking off with her parents. "It was none of it like this. You're dreaming your own dream. It was never any good."

THE DEEP GURGLING of my trache tube wakes me up. It feels as if it is hard to breathe, although the moisture is actually good for my lungs. I ring for a nurse, point to the blue tube. She drains it. "Now, go back to sleep," she says. That's useless. At 5:30 the aides come in to wash us. Why they have to come with their clammy rags and scrub our chilled bodies I cannot understand. Wouldn't it be better to let us sleep?

Nuala, I think, is still cozy under her linen sheets, under her down comforter. Sinead is dreaming at the foot of her bed. In an hour or so she'll wake and walk to the bathroom in her flannel pajamas. She'll run the hot water until the mirror is steamed over before she'll drop her pajamas and step into the shower. I think she likes to go in face first, soak her hair, and then turn to let the hot water stream down her thin back. She has six different shampoos lined up on a rack. She'll choose one, her first decision of the day. Then she'll soap her body. And some rare mornings perhaps she can't resist stroking herself between her legs with a soapy finger. When she does this, she never thinks of the boy who was killed. She imagines a man she's seen somewhere—at the Bells of Hell, on the streets, never at the hospital—but doesn't know. Or she thinks of no one at all, content with herself.

When she's had her pleasure she becomes a little depressed. She knows the rest of her morning will feel empty and without promise. This is what I imagine for Nuala.

I'M AWAKE when Nuala walks into the ward. Her shoes never squeak like some of the other nurses'; she can sneak up on you if you're not alert. But she always starts on the other side of the ward.

It's Brigit who comes in bouncing, trying to stir some life into us. As she brings her hands close to check my trache, I notice a tiny spot of blood between the first two fingers of her left hand. I catch her eye, then move mine there. I try to point. She pulls her hand away, grabbing a gauze pad from the table next to my bed and jamming it between her fingers. Then it seems that she spends longer than usual checking my IVs and my temperature, pulse, and pressure. She looks at me a little oddly. I see for the first time that her irises seem just slightly too small. Or maybe I just imagine this. How would I know how large her irises normally are?

"You're fine today, buster," she says quickly, smiling at me. "You're alert, very alert. That's good. What's my name?"

I mouth, Brigit.

"Yeah," she says. "What's your name?"

I mouth, Buster, and she bursts into laughter.

"When are we going out for that drink, buster?" she says.

I mouth, Tomorrow. Brigit laughs again and throws the gauze she's had between her fingers into the waste receptacle. She moves on to the Spanish lady in the room next to me, who is always restless and trying to climb out of bed. I don't know where she gets the strength. I lay for a while just staring at my purple Chuck Taylors, enjoying the quiet before Mrs. Mendoza (if she's awake today) turns on her Spanish-language TV station. God, I hate the sound of it.

Italian's what I like. When I dream about my great love affair, which I haven't had, it's always an Italian girl—dark or fair, Sicilian or Milanese, it doesn't matter. Very intelligent, very well educated. A little bit temperamental, a little contrite when she knows she's been awful. Talking to me only in Italian when we make love, walking around the house on hot days wearing only a thin silk slip. We'll live in Lucca, I think. We'll travel to Venice for Carnivale and wear masks and beautiful silk costumes. We'll become separated in the crowds and feel a huge loss, a devastation. But late in the evening, we'll find each other. We'll recognize each other despite the masks and all the others we've kissed and embraced through the evening, and we'll rush to each other like lovers who have been apart for months.

But today I'll have to listen to Mexican soap operas, unless Signora Mendoza's comatose or unless I wear my Walkman (which I hate, even when the music is beautiful, because it makes me feel even more cut off).

After lunch, Brigit comes over and sits on my bed. Nuala's busy outside the ward somewhere.

"What do you think you saw this morning?" she asks softly. I look into her eyes, willing my thoughts into her. Then I look at her hand and try to reach for it with my right hand. But she gives me hers. Gently I spread her fingers. I lightly touch the soft skin that connects them at the base. The marks are tiny, but they're whiter than the surrounding skin. She sees this and clenches her fist.

"It isn't what you think," she whispers, but I feel she is lying. "It's something I can't explain to you now. Someday, when your trache's out . . ." She laughs. "I'll tell you about it when you take me out for that drink. But for now it's a secret. OK? Our secret."

Sure, I mouth. She smiles broadly. She's good at reading my lips, better than Nuala. Suddenly I imagine sleeping with Brigit. I worry that I might not be able to get an erection. I never wake up with one anymore. Maybe I won't be able to do it. But Brigit would be kind, I think. She wouldn't let me feel embarrassed. We'd be there together, naked, laughing, and talking, and just holding each other. She's prettier than most of the women I went out with before I got sick, and I like her very much.

I wish there were someone I could ask about this absence of erections.

Later that day there's a small crisis. Mr. Dern, the old man on the other side of the ward, hasn't had a bowel movement in six days. They've given him enemas and suppositories, but they haven't worked. It's a pretty common problem. He's survived a heart attack, but now his diaphragm doesn't work and he can't breathe on his own, which is why he's here with the rest of us on The Machine. But he's always been the liveliest one. He can walk a few steps. You could see him alertly surveying the ward from his doorway.

So Betty, the head nurse, comes in wearing surgeon's greens. She's carrying a metal bowl, a jar of Vaseline, and what looks like a giant auger. I think it must be a medieval torture device. And it turns out to be not much less than that. They shut the curtains around Dern's bed, and I can tell by the rhythm of his groans that Betty is twisting her device up his rectum. There's a shout after a while. Betty emerges from behind the curtain with something awfully large in her metal bowl. It's wrapped in white paper. "We Roto-Rooter'd that one right out," she says to Brigit. She's smiling, and Brigit's laughing.

After a while they pulled the curtains back. Mr. Dern was lying on his side, but he looked as if he'd shrunken. He didn't move at all for the next two days, and when they helped him up and put him in his chair, his head lolled, like mine does most of the time. It looked like they'd taken most of the life out of him along with the intestinal blockage. But the nurses didn't seem to notice, as far as I could tell.

On an evening not long after that, I began to sweat. It was Nuala who noticed how pale I'd gone, how my gown was completely drenched. My eyes kept trying to roll back into my head. Jesus, another infection. "Temperature one-oh-four. Pulse one-twenty-five," Nuala said to Brigit. Above 104, brain cells shrivel and die.

"I'll get the doctor," Brigit said. Bells started ringing inside the little machines next to my bed. Voices seemed to have a strange echo. I couldn't keep a thought in my head. I could feel only the throbbing Machine. It seemed to be pumping too slowly. I began to wonder where I was, who these people around my bed were. Were they the bad girls who used to tie me down and stick me with needles? They stripped my bed and threw away my gown. I was naked, I was burning up, but I shivered when they put the ice blanket over me. Nuala put her cool hand on my cheek and said, "Don't go. Stay with us. Just stay with us."

I recognized Nuala. I wanted so much to stay, but I couldn't.

10

THE COMAS ARE NEVER LIKE DREAMS, in which you are always aware at some level that you're only asleep, even if they turn into nightmares. Being in a coma is like entering another world—when it's not just nothingness.

It isn't nothingness this time. It's much worse.

The Nevada sun was baking the corrugated tin airplane hangar where I was lying on a metal army cot. I didn't seem to be able to move anything but my right hand, and that only a little. I knew it was an airplane hangar, the kind they put up all over the West during World War II, because it was so huge I could barely see the ceiling. But the heat from the scorching metal roof was dropping down on me in heavy, suffocating waves. There was an open double door, and outside I could see rock and cactus, shadowless in white noon sun. I was burning up.

I could hear Glenn Miller's "I'll Be Seeing You." "In every lovely summer's day, in everything that's bright and gay/ I'll always think of you that way. . . ." How could the mechanics work in this heat? How could they replace a cracked manifold on a P-38? I was nude, and I knew if the temperature rose even a few degrees my blood and fluids would start to boil. I'd be cooked from the inside.

But I was certain that someone was getting an airplane ready for me. They were going to fly me out of this desert to an Air Corps hospital in California. I couldn't turn my head to see where they were doing this. I could hear the work and the cursing. But I could only look straight down past my toes, where there seemed to be a lunch counter lined with stools: chrome columns with round bright-red Naugahyde seats. On the counter there were a few clear-plastic cake and pie holders. And behind it were big chrome coffee machines, chrome milk shake mixers, and a big red Coke fountain. Two or three of my Jamaican friends were behind the counter too, their hair in dreadlocks. They were wearing khaki Air Corps overalls and masses of colorful little beads, every color you could imagine: indigo, carmine, chrome yellow, scarlet, plum, robin's egg blue, orange, burnt umber, turquoise, hot pink, acid green. Not regulation issue, I was sure. The girls were all fat, and dancing to Glenn Miller's swing tune as if it were Bob Marley.

My eyes kept going back to the red Coke machine. I stared at it for days. It always looked the same because the sun never changed position; I could see that from the shadowless desert outside. The Jamaicans were dancing and laughing. There was nobody else in the hangar as far as I could tell, except the mechanics who were somewhere behind me working on the plane.

For two days I banged my right knuckles against the iron frame of my cot, hoping that rapping might attract someone's attention. My skin was covered with dust, my face was unshaven and itchy, and sweat was flushing the grit on my forehead into my eyes. Nobody came.

For three more days and two more nights I rapped with my knuckles as hard as I could. My knuckles were swollen to the size of marbles. The skin was scraped completely off, but there wasn't any blood because I was down to bare white bone. My mouth was almost blocked by my dry swollen tongue. I knew if I could see it, my tongue would be black. I tried to breathe through my nose. My mouth was drier than the driest desert in the world. My teeth were all loose because my gums had shrunken from dehydration. I started to cry but there wasn't enough moisture in my body to form tears. I kept banging. I knew that if someone didn't bring me a drink I would die of thirst any minute. Coke, a glass of orange juice, a glass of water would save my life. The bones of my knuckles began to chip away, flake by flake.

I lay dying in that hot cot, helpless, when I could see behind the counter good things to drink, and three women who I thought were friends. Maybe I was already dead, that's why they never heard my rapping or seemed to see me there in the middle of that roasting hangar. Suddenly the fat, round face of my best Jamaican friend appeared within inches of mine. She glistened with sweat. She took my right hand to stop my rapping. I didn't feel any pain; I was too consumed with thirst. "Hush now," she said. "Don't be making no racket. I know you thirsty. I know you think you could drink a river, man. But you can't drink nothing. Not a drop. Because of your condition. You know this. You been living this for a month. Don't you think I'd give you something if I could?

"Bear up, man. You got to bear up, and bear it. You by the rivers of Babylon now, but they not for you to drink. Only pray, now. Jah do what He will."

Dry, so dry.

As parched and desiccated as if I'd been buried for 3,000 years, like an ancient Egyptian, even my mouth stuffed full of sand.

SUDDENLY I'M FLOATING, weightless in frigid black space, a stray piece of matter in the cosmos. I see the arched shoulder of Orion, the sinister string of stars known as Draco. I am sure I can feel the caress of a gentle solar wind against my skin. The gamma rays pass painlessly through me. I feel so far away from anything solid. I see bright flashes like shooting stars, but there are no shooting stars in airless space. It must be electrical misfirings in my brain.

In the midst of this celestial isolation I suddenly hear Nuala's bitter voice whispering inside my head. It's about to go all wrong for me. I know it.

"You know I stay with you as long as I can. I talk to you and touch you, try to bring you back," she's saying. "I tell you stories of my life, the gossip about Brigit and the others. I read poems. But you never even blink, you son of a bitch.

"I'm drained, I'm cracking. But you wouldn't care. I'm getting into trouble with my supervisors. They say, 'Nuala, you're wasting time. Work with patients who have a chance.'

"You have a chance. I goddamn know you do. But the way you keep going away is breaking me. You get so close to being well, and then you fall off the cliff again."

Once more I'm drifting in the solar wind, hearing nothing but a thin distant hum of stars burning themselves out, a faint whirring of galaxies rotating. I float and rotate too. But slowly Nuala's accusing whispers return, though they seem gentler now, and sadder.

"I went to a bar with Brigit last night. She wanted to hear Black 47 scream about how much they hate the English. She says there's nothing like dancing to hatred. A really nice-looking fella started buying the beers. And all I could talk about was this patient I have who keeps slipping into comas. He got bored after a while; I could see his eyes scanning the room. Black 47 was working up a real sweat, and the talking died. He excused himself when the band took a break. He never even asked for my phone number. I'd have given it to him too.

"And you, you bastard, you lie there. How did you get your hooks into me? It's the first thing you learn in training: Never get emotionally involved with patients.

"Brigit just laughs at me. She danced her ass off, and when I left there were two guys arguing about who should give her a ride home. She thinks it's funny I could mess up so badly. She keeps to herself enough. All that flirting? It's forgotten as soon as she goes off duty.

"This has never happened to me before. You won't leave me alone. I think you come into my dreams on purpose. Who invited you? Who wants you? Stay out, you."

MY EYES OPEN. I can't focus at first, in the dim light. It must be the middle of the night. My right hand is heavily bandaged. There's not a soul in my room. But there's a chair pulled close to my bed, and I can see a depression in the cushion where someone's recently been sitting.

If I could touch the seat of the chair, I believe it would still be warm.

11

"I'VE BEEN READING the medical texts on you," Nuala says brightly the next morning when she comes into my room. I think it's the next, anyway. It could be any morning. It could be days and days later. At first I'm not certain I've returned, but I recognize my things and my wild-haired nurse. "Poring over the stuff the doctors use for reference. And don't think I don't understand it, mister. I'm a better diagnostician than most third-year residents. And guess what? I can't find any examples of patients who've ever experienced your peculiar combinations of pneumonias, septicemias, and comas.

"That," she says, "makes you one odd fish. You're a complete enigma to everyone here. Bet you sort of like that, don't you?"

Rather be average, I mouth. And understandable at least to myself, I add in my mind.

"I don't think you could stand being ordinary, Mr. Blatchley," Nuala says.

What have I done now? I mouth back.

Nuala just laughs. "You know. You're a dangerous fella, or you'd like people to think so."

THINGS HAD HAPPENED I could never understand. And a bad thing had happened when I was gone. Brigit had to tell me all about it. She seemed more friendly than she'd ever been, maybe because of my close call. Or maybe she was worried about our secret.

The old man Betty had Roto-rooter'd died. Perforated bowel, massive infection no known drugs could defeat. There was no connection between him and me, but I always felt one whenever anybody died. My mind was working that way then; things seemed linked and locked. I'd become superstitious, maybe even a little suspicious. Everything seemed to have many layers, multiple meanings. There was no such thing as a clear, straightforward answer. And it was harder and harder to know if it was just the drugs or some new pathways in my mind.

I even wondered why Clare hadn't been to see me, without considering that I wouldn't have known if she had, since I was unconscious.

———

BRIGIT WAS SO EXCITED she was practically bouncing as she sat on the edge of my bed later that day. Nuala had a boyfriend at last. She'd met him a week ago (while I was in Nevada) at the Bells of Hell. Brigit had picked him up, naturally, but judged him perfect for Nuala and passed him on in that way girls are so good at. He was a reporter at the *Post*—an Australian but not a rough one, one with some polish and sensibility. A good Melbourne family. "Nuala's a little bit over the moon," Brigit told me. "This is such a good thing."

I don't know what I expected to feel, but I got a hollowness in my stomach. I told myself it was just a reaction to my last check-out, to the fact that I never seemed to get much better. I was more worried now about simple survival, not just how damaged I might be when I got better. The "when" suddenly seemed to be in doubt. As did my making a world for Nuala. It occurred to me for the first time that maybe Nuala had no need of such a thing, wouldn't want it, would be offended if she knew about it. Maybe my help was no help at all, just dreams, just a way to make myself feel useful. Because lying here weak and sick certainly didn't inspire me.

Just before I passed out this last time I remember that Nuala had asked me not to go. Surely that meant something. Or maybe she hadn't actually said it. Maybe I just imagined it.

But Nuala seemed warmer after her little medical lecture. She smiled and chatted more. She even told me about Sinead. She was a wild woman of a dog, with so much energy and an eye for the boys already. "Like Brigit," she said.

I choked a little laugh.

"And she really is good company, despite what I said at first."

I gave her a weak smile, to say don't worry about it. I was hoping she'd say more, but she didn't.

Every day I try to save my mind for Nuala; she's the one I want to talk to. I try to read. I can't handle anything serious because of my poor attention span and the ease with which I'm confused. I get Clare to bring me some easy things—John Grisham, John le Carré, things I've read before. I'm trying to follow *Smiley's People*, which I already know almost by heart, but I can't get past a page at a time. I try to rip the book in half, but I'm not strong enough.

Brigit walks in while I'm trying. "If you really want, I'll rip it for you," she says. "But you don't. You're frustrated. It isn't your brain. It's all those gallons of drugs we're pumping into you. Trust me. When the drugs go down, the brain'll come right back."

I didn't realize that she was lying. I didn't know then that not a single doctor in that hospital, not even the top neurologist, knew what kind of consciousness I'd have if I survived. I didn't know either that the betting was ten to one that I'd leave this room in a body bag.

WHAT I WANT MOST in the world now is to talk to my grandfather, buried more than twenty years ago. Who knows if he's anywhere at all in any form? That's part of what I'd like to ask him. But really I want to know how it feels at the moment of death. Do you realize it's the end, or does your brain flood itself with chemicals to ease the passage, to disguise the horror and finality? Is it frightening or peaceful? Or is it a wild brawl you know you have lost long before it ends? Is there any point in what Dylan Thomas said: "Rage, rage against the dying of the light"?

I don't know that I'll necessarily die soon. But I want some answers in advance. I've been that way all my life—full of questions as a kid, driving my grandfather crazy. I would have been the same with my father if I'd had the chance, but I rarely saw him; he was always working, and then one morning he dropped dead in front of me. Coronary. I was fourteen. I remember only one private conversation with my dad. He and I were driving out into the woods to gather wild holly and greens for Christmas decorations. I was sitting in the front seat of his '52 Ford two-door sedan. I wasn't more than six or seven. I could barely see over the dashboard. I was nervous alone with him; I hunched against the door on my side to put the greatest distance between us. But he was cheerful and whistling and pointing out things—the red horse with wings above the Mobil gas station, the real horses in a paddock on the roadside.

Finally I asked my big question: "Why did you marry Mom?"

He laughed and said, "Because I loved her."

"That's it? When you love someone you just marry them and have kids and buy a house to live in?"

"Yep, it's that simple. It was that simple. But you kids grow up so fast. I remember when I could hold you in the palm of my hand."

"You can't even pick me up now. I'm too big."

"Bet you a milk shake when we stop I can grab you by the belt and pick you off the ground with one arm," my father said.

He did. But we were running late on the way home so I never got the milk shake.

Every day I'm awake I test myself with things like that. First I try to remember my great-grandfather's name. Then my grandfather's and his face and voice. Then my father's and his face and voice. I can still see and hear my grandfather, but my father is just a name—and a handful of words in a voice I don't recognize.

WHAT'S UP? I mouthed to Brigit. I felt warm in my heart toward her.

"We're going to the Bells after work. Nuala's meeting Ian and I'm meeting my new fellow. I forget his name—it's Bob, I think. He's American, of course," Brigit said. She'd been gone from the ward for a while and her eyes were bright. She was clenching her left fist. I frowned at it. "Our secret," she said. "Don't worry, I know what I'm doing. I'm a registered nurse, remember?" This sent her into gales of laughter. I wished all the dope I was getting would make me laugh so hard. All it did was keep me from spinning off into some universe of pain and insanity. Of course, maybe that's what it was doing for Brigit too.

The sleeping drugs were useless again that night. I was having a lot of pain in my joints. I was constantly aware of the whoomph and gush of The Machine too. You had to be, knowing that if the sound stopped you'd be dead in five minutes.

I didn't bother trying to picture the people I knew best. It's too predictable; the mind always comes back to a handful of indelible images. I know I'll see Joe Cigna, my friend in Homicide, sit down at his steel desk like he does every morning with a cup of coffee and a jelly donut, which he'll consume in three huge bites. He'll leave a dusting of powdered sugar all over the front of his pants. It'll be five or ten phone calls before he notices it. Then he'll say shit, stand up, and try to brush it all off with his hands. Same with Clare. I know her routines so well, how she'll rush home from the broadcast studio and phone Nick and Alexandra, and the beautiful girl I call The Alien, and Raphael and her latest protégé to find out where they're all going to go that night. Then she'll spend too long getting dressed and arrive late at wherever it is.

So I tried thinking about Brigit and Nuala in the Bells of Hell with their boys. It's a homey sort of bar with sawdust on the floor, a dartboard, the jukebox up to date, except for Peter's Sex Pistols fixation. You could get a good hamburger there. I wondered what it would be like to have a good hamburger again. Not one thing had been in my mouth for more than six weeks except these awful minty foam-rubber swabs they used to clean my teeth. I didn't even get to rinse afterward. My chest just rose and fell with The Machine, leaving my mouth useless. They may as well have sewn it shut; it would have saved everyone the trouble of trying to read my lips. Really that was the only use, and I couldn't say anything worthwhile—just beg for a suctioning or ask for more drugs that I never got.

I was lying there around midnight, thinking how Nuala would look as she bit into a specially juicy cheeseburger, when a tremendous spring thunderstorm broke. My ward was on the tenth floor; I was next to the window and I had a fine city view. The bolts looked like they were crashing right into the taller buildings over near the river. My pulse picked up every time there was a flash, a crack, and a rumble of thunder. I would've liked to be sitting next to Nuala somewhere cozy, my arm around her shoulder, drinking a glass of Chateau Trotanoy while we watched the storm. She's not the type to be scared of storms; she'd love them the way I did.

But Nuala was surely watching the storm in a better way by now. No flannel pajamas that night. The lightning flashing through the skylight of her apartment would show a man lying flat on his back on Nuala's linen sheets. And Nuala sitting on him, her naked back bluish in the lightning and her hair loose and wild and electric red, gently posting up and down. He'd reach up to stroke her breasts. But she'd push his hands away, place her own on his knees, and lean back, her face turned up toward the skylight. This was as clear to me as if I was in the room with them, each blast of lightning freezing a frame. I wanted so much to be the man on Nuala's linens, deny it how I would. That's what making my world for Nuala actually came down to. I felt ashamed. I'd been pitying her. But at least for a while it had kept me from pitying myself.

It was Nuala who had the life, the world, the control. She didn't need me, with my nothing, my stupid dog idea, my picture-postcard Ireland, my imaginary memories of a little redhead squealing with delight in her grandda's curragh.

NEXT MORNING I was searching for signs, for evidence, like a jealous adolescent. Nuala looked untouched. She looked exactly as she always did; even the wisps of hair that habitually strayed were the same wisps as always. She looked rested, like she'd slept long and well. She asked if I'd seen the storm. I nodded. "Lovely, wasn't it?" she said. "Your pulse is a little fast this morning. How's your breathing?" She looked closely into my eyes, and I saw myself reflected in hers: too thin, greasy-haired, pasty. Not a specimen anyone would choose, even as a softened reflection in the green of Nuala's eyes.

"You know, when you get off the ventilator, Brigit and I are going to wheel you down to the Bells of Hell to celebrate. You can get a pass to leave for a few hours once you're free of The Machine," she said. "We'll take you in a wheelchair."

"Don't know if I want to take him anywhere," Brigit said as she walked in. "He's American. They're big trouble. Just ask me."

"Well?" Nuala said.

"If you ever meet an American named Bob, claims to do something on Wall Street, claims he's being driven crazy by the shape of your lips, all he can think of is kissing them, run like hell the other way. That's all I'll say," Brigit said. "Except that you better be faster on your feet than I am after four Guinnesses."

"Well?" Nuala said.

"Well, it's a good thing Peter is a gentleman and runs a respectable bar, or this Bob would have had my skirt up around my head right on the pool table."

Nuala began to laugh so hard she seemed on the verge of

hysteria. Her laughter began to wake up the drowsy, drugged patients in the other rooms. I'd never seen Nuala laugh so wildly.

"Only go to movies with men and then straight home. That's my advice to you," Nuala said. "Then put on your flannel pajamas and climb into bed by yourself."

"Get out," Brigit said. "You're up to a bit more than that these days."

"Am not," Nuala said. "I'm a saint. Saint Nuala. Everyone knows that. Ask Ian."

"But he's Australian!"

"So?"

"Never get a straight answer out of an Australian. If he did ya, he'd swear to God you're a virgin, and if he didn't do ya, he'd swear to his mates that you were the hottest sheila he'd ever met, practically raped him when he went to shake your hand good night."

"Now, Nurse Brigit, calm down. Can't you see you're disturbing the patients, especially this one here?" Nuala said. My clawlike left hand was shaking, and my Chuck Taylors were flexing at the toes. They both started laughing at me. I grinned as well as I could, but the new wound from the steel drainage tube they'd rammed into my upper left chest after the last time I went out was hurting pretty bad. Cold steel in your flesh is so alien that you never get used to it.

Later, when things were slow, Brigit came into my room. I

looked at her left hand, and then mouthed: You gave Bob fentanyl. Jesus, chances you take.

She paled immediately but seemed too stunned to say anything. I mouthed, very slowly, desperate for her to understand: Take care. Beg. Care for you. Please.

She nodded and walked right out of the ward.

12

SEE WHAT I'VE MADE for Nuala, anyway. Or for
myself. Does it matter either way? I've made the
broad stone steps leading from the Venice railroad
station down to the canal. I've made the richly polished mahogany water taxi that will take us along that
canal halfway to the sea. There are brightly colored
strings of lights outlining the restaurants. Torches
flame at the entrances of certain palazzos where balls
and revelries must fill the grand salons with music,
laughter. In the sky just above the silhouettes of the
palazzos and black water sparkling with colored lights,
a full moon the color of old gold is being eclipsed. We
are sailing along its diminishing old gold path in the
waters.

Nuala has never been to Venice before. She's

never been welcomed into the red and gold splendor of the Hotel Danieli, never dined on razor shells, langoustine, the perfectly white flesh and black skins of grilled eels. She hasn't tasted the dry Kraj wine from Cormons, nor the slightly sweet Picolit from the Collio that I have ordered for our room. We stand on our balcony watching the gold moon reappear, sipping the Picolit. She has never taken off her clothes and lain with me on the linen sheets in the Hotel Danieli. She has never before lowered herself on me. There is a sixteenth-century armoire that runs the length of the wall next to the bed. Its carved walnut doors are mirrored. She's never been able to see herself the way she can now. She's never watched her own face as she comes. Now, rising lightly in a city afloat, she sees it, gilded in Venetian moonlight.

SUDDENLY I'M BLINDED by white light. There's a chrome gurney next to my bed. Two nurses are removing my blue tube from The Machine and attaching it to a blue tank under the gurney. Then they unplug IVs and plug in others on stands with wheels. Two strong black orderlies lift my bottom sheet, raise me, and place me on the gurney. "Let's go, let's go," a doctor insists.

We're racing down the ward, the two black men practically trotting, the nurses pushing the IV stands struggling to keep up. We're clear of the ward and out into the maze of the hospital. We squeeze, all of us, into a stainless steel elevator that drops with amazing speed and actually bounces when it stops. Then we're racing down corridors again, the strips of fluorescent lighting overhead blurring. There are no windows anywhere. There are doors the color of surgeon's greens concealing rooms I've never seen. Corridors end at blank walls.

Then we're in a dark, cold towering room. There is a booth on one end lit up in colors like an air traffic control center. They lift my sheet again and put me on a steel rack. They slide the rack into a polished steel tube so small that I'm sure I will not fit. But I do. My breath condenses on the steel just inches from my face; my shoulders touch cold metal. I'm shivering. My shoulders recoil from the steel. A coffin must have more room. Everyone leaves the tube room and goes into the control center. I'm wondering why my mother isn't here. Where can she be? Where's my Nuala, my Clare, my Brigit? Why am I here to face this alone?

Then I hear the pings, the creaking, and more pings that sound like the sonar signals in movies about submarines. I suddenly realize it's just the CAT scanner. It's a great relief. They are only having a look at my lungs. Let them. They'll see the scars and air pockets, the usual signs of my disease. The urgency has alarmed me, but then I remember the CAT scanner is heavily used; it never stops. People are shoved into it at all hours of the day and night, whenever there's a slot, even if you are in Venice with Nuala. They don't care where you are; you are there at the sufferance of The

Machine. The pinging lasts and lasts and lasts, and so does my shivering. Perhaps a half hour passes; it's hard to know. Pain stiffens my shoulders and hips; my wasted ass is sore almost beyond bearing. A voice comes over the speaker in the tube: "You're breathing too fast. Stay calm. Not much longer now. Breathe as normally as you can."

I learn that night you can resist The Machine. You do not have to do exactly as it demands; you can go a little bit faster or a little bit slower than it wants you to. I clutch this knowledge closely; I cling to this tiny hope of control.

I'm calm on the ride back upstairs. Nobody says anything to me about how it went. Some expert will analyze it in the morning. Unless something big has changed in the last week, he will see a lot of rotten infected tissue in the lower lobe of my right lung, and air pockets near the top, and already scar tissue where the earliest infections have healed. There will be a debate among the doctors about whether to cut out that lower lobe. The surgeon will be for it all the way. The pulmonary specialist and the infectious disease specialist will argue that they ought to be given more of a chance. The pulmonary specialist periodically drains me; I have a row of holes up my right side already. The infectious disease man has new combinations of very new antibiotics he wants to try on my drug-resistant bacteria.

I keep track of all this as best I can. I try to stay current with what's what, another exercise to keep hold of my mind. But only in flashes of clarity, when I'm not drifting in my fuzzy, druggy state, or confused by the effects of new combinations of drugs, or just too sick to think clearly at all.

I DON'T DREAM ANY MORE that night. But I'm not certain I sleep either. I hear pinging. I see tiny red and green lights on a box next to my bed. I hear the wet, hissing voices of my blue tube. They're speaking to me of things I don't understand. Back into my mind comes the vision of the girl with the transparent skin. Her exposed lungs are fresh. They whisper, a feathery sound, not like the rasping, sucking sound my own make.

It seems very early in the morning when Brigit comes fussing around my bed. "Scanned you last night, didn't they? You're gonna be in the *Guinness Book of World Records* pretty soon. As of today you've got the record for this ICU: forty-two days and still kicking. You are one tough son of a bitch, buster."

"Let's see how tough." I hear another voice, and my heart sinks. It really does; it drops lower in my chest, and all the atrophied muscles in my legs tighten in apprehension. It's Cindy, the electricity enthusiast. She jokes about what she does; she calls it Pain and Torture. "We're going to get you to walk a little today."

I look at Brigit, but she's just smiling at me.

Cindy's a strange sort. She gets you into all sorts of positions and when your gown falls open she yells at you. "Come on, we don't need any old flashers around here." As if there's anything you could do about it. As if she's never seen one. She's got masses of curly black hair, a strong curved nose, and the perfectly proportioned body of a gymnast. She's only about five feet two but she's stronger than you could believe; she's borne my entire weight, which admittedly isn't what it used to be but is certainly thirty or forty pounds more than she weighs. She's got a regular boyfriend, and I'd bet she's had more than her share before this one.

The drill is this: Cindy and Brigit place their hands behind my back and help raise me to a sitting position, my stick legs dangling over the edge of the bed. I feel insecure, sure if I tumble forward nothing will stop me from hitting the floor. Knowing this, they like to let me sit there on my own for a while, not touching me, telling me to sit up straight whenever my aching back begins to slouch.

Then Cindy brings over a four-legged aluminum walker with rubber tips on each leg. I put my hands on the handles, and they help me stand up. I find I have to support almost all my weight with my arms, which is hard since my left one ends in a claw that has almost no strength. Then Cindy backs up about five feet and says, "Walk to me. Move the walker a few inches forward with your arms and take a step." It always feels like my blue tube and the IVs are in the way but they aren't; Brigit's seen to that. I take a step and it feels suddenly like red-hot rods of pig iron have been laid up against the backs of my legs. They tremble and burn. It's the worst pain I experience in this place. My arms are shaking uncontrollably. Another step, the same red-hot pain. "You're incredibly tight after all this time on your back; the ligaments are just tight," Cindy says. "We've gotta stretch them, and then you'll be able to move around and start getting your strength back." I take another step and start trembling so much that Cindy grabs me around the waist and shoulder and eases me back to bed. I feel exhausted. It's a struggle to keep my eyes dry and my face composed.

"Well, not so tough after all," Cindy says. "Next time it's five full steps, or I'll let you stand there 'til you fall."

Lying down, I smile at her and we shake hands. She's got a great strong grip. I know she wouldn't drop me.

Nuala stuck her head in my room once to say hello, but I saw nothing else of her that day. They increased the intervals of my fentanyl drip that afternoon because they'd figured out there had been a tolerance buildup. I liked it. It didn't make me feel high, but it seemed to make all the synapses in my brain fire more gently, less raggedly. It suppressed the sparks, the shooting stars. I felt less clearheaded but also less like I was losing my mind. I did have a few moments of drugged fear that Nuala knew about the world I had made for her last night, a brief irrational period in which it seemed that Venice had been real to her as well.

"Resting comfortably." That's how they'd describe me that afternoon. I tried another page of *Smiley's People*, but it wasn't much better. And I hated to watch the TV; it made me feel sicker and depressed.

It was really just bad luck that had brought me to this. Brigit, who wasn't as discreet as the hospital would have her be, said, "Jesus, we were all sure you were HIV, serious AIDS, when you checked in. We're not supposed to test without the patient's permission but you were too out of it to ask. We've got to do it, for our own protection and to know what we're dealing with. People couldn't believe you were negative. They did three separate tests."

"You were so bad, all Dr. Matahai could say was 'poor fuck!' when he saw your chart. We all cracked up. Imagine calling a patient 'poor fuck'!" She laughed.

EARLY THAT EVENING Clare came by. She was all in black: short black skirt, black sweater, black heels. Bright red lipstick. It seemed like I hadn't seen her in so long. MISSED YOU, I pointed on the alphabet board.

"I'm sorry, I've just been so busy at work. And you were in a coma. I called every day to get your condition though."

WHAT IS IT?

"Still critical. That's why you're still in the ICU."

WHAT NEW YOU?

"Oh, my life is crazy. They're making a lot of changes at work, and Kerry's husband has left her. I've been spending a lot of evenings with her, talking it out. A bunch of us have been going to different bars. Don't look at me in that sad way. I've come as often as I could; it's been over a month. I think about you every day. I call to see how you are. But I can't sit here every night and hold your hand."

Why does she sound so cross?

FRIENDS? I point out on the board.

"Yes, great friends, the best friends. I'd do anything for you, but I've got to get on with my own life too, haven't I?"

LONELY.

"Oh, please, don't crack my heart. Not that you're trying to, but you know what I mean. I know it must be awful for you here, alone and worried and in pain. I'll come as often as I can. Just not every night, OK? Please understand. I care for you so much, but this is more than I can bear."

OK.

"Really OK?"

YES. ALWAYS HAPPY. MAKING A WORLD.

"Making a world? What are you talking about?"

NICE WORLD IN MY HEAD.

13

I NEVER SHOULD HAVE BEEN HERE in this wretched bed, tapped, tubed, and wasting. It didn't have to happen. I could've caught chicken pox like most every child. I didn't have to catch it on a New York subway (that's the doctors' theory, since I certainly hadn't been around any children). It shouldn't have gone beyond the normal fever and the rash. My varicella virus shouldn't have filled my lungs with phlegm and pus and nearly killed me that first week with its assault on my spinal cord and brain. It shouldn't have poisoned my blood, almost to the point of death. It doesn't usually.

But it did these things to me.

And when the virus was defeated, it left behind neurological damage that paralyzed my diaphragm.

I could not breathe one breath on my own. That's when they slit my throat and hooked me up to The Machine.

They want you off The Machine as soon as they can do it. They don't say why; it seems a sensible course of recovery, so nobody asks. But there are other reasons.

The Machine that keeps you alive, with its clockwork huffs and watery voices, is also The Machine that is likely to kill you.

Every hospital in the world comes to harbor deadly bacteria that shrug off the usual antibiotics. They're impossible to exterminate, filter, or defeat because they're constantly mutating. They can always find ways to insinuate themselves into the pulsing red wetness of your most vulnerable interiors.

That is what they are so worried about in my case, Brigit tells me. Two or three kinds of pneumonia have tried but failed to kill me since the varicella was beaten. I go unconscious; I come back from comas and nobody knows what permanent damage may have been done to my nervous system, my brain. They know my lungs are wrecked, scarred, and full of holes. They hope for the healing of these wounds. But I'm at risk every day that the blue tube remains attached to the plug in my throat, and no one knows when my diaphragm will start up properly again.

I've become a famous case, Nuala tells me. A lot of doctors I've never seen before show up in my room to have a look at me and my charts. "For curiosity," Nuala says. "They don't have anything to do with your treatment. You have your own team of specialists for that."

Nuala has bad news. I can tell by the way her eyes won't hold mine. They slide too easily off to the side, even as she holds my hand.

"We're supposed to tell everyone they're doing fine, that they'll be leaving before they know it. They mostly leave in body bags."

I want truth, I mouth.

"This is very hard for me. It's a hard thing to tell," Nuala says, rising from her chair to pour bitter orange fluid into the pouch that's attached to my nose tube. "Your system is supposed to have been overwhelmed by all those bugs, a kind of toxic shock. Or else your lungs or heart or kidneys were supposed to quit. All our smart doctors can't quite figure out why you're still here. They're basically experimenting and waiting to see what happens."

Ah, fuck it, I mouth. I'm tired.

She finishes pouring in the fluid. I can taste it now in the back of my throat. "Of course you are. But you keep fighting to stay in this world in ways the doctors can't fathom."

She suddenly smiles at me. "I know why, of course: You're just so crazy about me and Brigit you couldn't bear to part from us. Right?"

Right.

Maybe not directly, but surely I have been hanging on for some reason. Maybe at first it was Clare—the friendship, the one connection that seemed to have brightened my life. I thought it was good forever, but that's changing now, isn't it? She's already distancing herself to ease the pain. But what else is there? I have so few friends. I don't have a particularly glowing future. No family to speak of. Grandparents dead, parents dead, no center of gravity to keep my brother and sister and me from spinning off on the arcs of careers, of lives that move farther and farther apart with each year. We're rarely in touch; our birthday and Christmas phone calls have stopped. It will be a mighty small funeral. So now maybe it is only Brigit and Nuala, Nuala and what I'm making for her, that keep me from giving up. Maybe I'll know if I check out for good. That's probably the only time you get all the answers, if you ever do at all.

MOST OF THE PEOPLE in the ICU leave near dawn.

Sometimes their kidneys give up, their livers stop filtering, their hearts fail to pump, they have strokes, or they are flattened by hordes of bacteria. There's sufficient virulence lurking around to take down even the strong ones. Usually they die very early in the morning, 3:00 or 4:00 or 5:00, when life is at its lowest ebb.

But I'm the famous patient. The one who never dies and never gets better. Every nurse and orderly and doctor greets me by name. Nurses come into my room when they think I'm asleep to have a private gossip. They know I won't get upset if I awake and see them there. Brigit and Nuala and I are getting to be like old companions. Sometimes we even talk about the things we'll do together this week or the week after, all of us ignoring the fact that I'm not apparently going anywhere at all, that I can't walk a step on my own, and that I'm never actually speaking, just mouthing words.

On my fiftieth day in the ICU, something very odd happens. Two men are better enough to be scheduled for transfer to normal wards that day. There's a positive attitude throughout the ICU. I can feel it.

But six other people suddenly die. It seems to take the orderlies hours to stuff them into body bags and run them down to the morgue for autopsies, though they're really very efficient. But six in one day is a lot, especially when they all die in the early morning. Even Brigit looks frazzled and worn; Nuala's pale and moving very slowly by lunch. They expect to lose most of their patients, but so many at once is shocking.

The slaughter leaves me in my corner room and two women way down at the other end of the ward. The hospital decides to send a psychologist to each of us, to find out how we are taking the terrible news. Doesn't bother me. This is place to die, I mouthed.

"A race to cry?" he said.

I repeated, Place to die.

"No," he said, "it's a place to get better. Everything that can be done is done."

Sure, I mouthed. I'm gonna walk out here in day or two myself.

"It's good to have a healthy attitude," he said.

That was the extent of our visit.

"Nualala, Nualala," Brigit called out when the psychologist had gone off to more hopeful precincts, not, I trusted, too depressed by our little Death Row. "We're going to have it so easy for a while, unless we get some new patients. Just our old man over there, the one who loves us so much he refuses to go."

I gesture for the alphabet board over against the wall. Now there is time for the alphabet board. Brigit hands it to me.

YOU'RE BABES. WANT YOU BOTH, I point.

Nuala is giggling, and Brigit has the cheek to sashay over to my bed, sit on the edge near the drainage tubes coming out of my chest, and bend over to whisper in my ear. I can just feel the light touch of one of her breasts on my shoulder as she says, "Already told you once. Wait'll you get out of here, buster."

CAN'T WAIT MUCH LONGER, I point.

"Oh, I think you can last awhile longer," Brigit says, glancing at where the sheet lay absolutely flat over my groin, no sign of anything stirring. "But that's good. You'll appreciate it more."

"Brigit, give the poor man a break," Nuala says. There is an edge in her voice. "This isn't the Bells, girl."

That night after quitting hours, Nuala comes in and sits in the visitor's chair, takes her shoes off, and rests her feet on the bed. "Brigit's already gone off. But I'm too tired for the Bells tonight. I wish I could get a foot massage."

I hold up my left claw and grin to show that my spirit is willing. The night nurse has already checked all my signs and given me my medication. And for once, damn it, it seems to be kicking in. A warmth is spreading up through my legs from my feet and into my belly and chest. It's dim in the room. Nuala's big green eyes look almost black.

"It's hard for you, isn't it, that we talk to you and you have such a hard time letting us know what you're thinking?"

Frustrating, I mouth. Love to talk.

"Love to listen, too?" Nuala asks.

I nod.

"I've some stories to tell, no one to tell them to. Maybe sometime I could tell you?"

My pleasure, I mouth. But my breathing's getting a bit raspy, these watery voices are creeping into my ears, and I'm sinking down into them. All I can see is Nuala's big dark eyes. She puts the back of her hand on my forehead; she wipes my face with a washcloth. Then she reaches down and unplugs the blue tube. All I can watch is her eyes, but I feel her gently insert the suction tube, and I hear the harsh sucking of thick mucus. Her face is so close I could almost kiss her, if I could raise my head. I feel embarrassed at what she must see coming out that suction tube.

"WHEN I HAD FREE TIME at nursing school, and Brigit was off at a pub or a dance, I liked to take long walks to the outskirts of the city," Nuala tells me. "In the middle of acres and acres of the greenest grass you ever saw were a bunch of ten-story concrete tenements. The damp patches running down the walls made them look like they were weeping, even in the sun. This was where the government warehoused the unemployed, the unemployable, and the working poor, when the inner city slums crumbled beyond repair.

"And all around these concrete towers and all over the green grass roamed hundreds of horses," Nuala goes on. "No one could say how it had begun, but for years the tenement boys had been acquiring horses. The trading market was cheap, the upkeep nothing; there were no stables, no oats or hay. The horses just grazed the empty acres. Saddles were too expensive to buy and too big to nick, but it was no special trick to walk out of a tack shop with a good bit and bridle under your windbreaker."

Nuala says she'd watch lads of twelve and thirteen and fourteen wildly galloping their horses bareback, wheeling and pirouetting like hussars, racing one another in packs around the green grounds. Some of them were on heroin already; some sold it and had strings of horses, not just one. Most had had brushes with the law.

"But I imagined an encampment of nomads," Nuala says. "And even the tenement towers in the background couldn't spoil my illusion. There were just these young Tartars on an Asian steppe, flying before the wind."

She found it the saddest and most beautiful sight she ever saw in Dublin.

Sometimes a bold one would canter up to her, offer to sell her heroin, in an accent she could scarcely penetrate. She'd try to talk to them about their mounts, but the boys knew at the first few words she wasn't one of their lot, and they would quickly wheel and gallop back to their mates.

"The authorities," Nuala says, "were always telling the newspapers they had plans to do something about all this horse business. So were the animal-protection groups. They said it was a scandal that those poor horses should be treated so cruelly. Cruelty to animals was something they could not abide."

NOW NUALA'S JUST LOOKING in my eyes, watching my lids droop, watching the faint smile fade from my face. She puts on her shoes. I reach out with my right hand for her hand. She takes it and kisses it and lays it across my chest, so the IVs won't pinch me in the night.

"I'll tell you more another time," she says. "Dream well."

I'm gone before she is.

14

"JESUS, what's happened to your beautiful veins?" I hear Brigit crooning first thing one morning. "They're gone, gone, all faded away." All her wrapping of the rubber band and tapping to find a useful vein have roused me. "I need your blood, love," Brigit says when she sees I am awake. "Not so easy with your veins collapsed. If I were a vampire, I'd take you back to the store."

Finally she finds one in the back, on my elbow, and draws a vial. "Look how easy I'd be," she says, showing me her pale inner forearm laced with a pale-blue tracery. But what runs so dangerously through those fragile tubes? Can you see the end of her in them, like a palm reader gauging a lifeline? I grab her wrist. She makes a fist. "No, no," she says. "You promised. I'm careful. You can see I'm all right."

She looks better than all right. She looks full of life. What's up? New boy? I mouth.

"Not new, just Bob. He turned out to be just as ready to put my skirt over my head and my panties down around my ankles in the privacy of my own home, without any stimulants. He's a lot of fun, he is!" she crows. "Puts a spring in my step every morning."

Nuala's Aussie?

"Now that's really her business. I can't say her secrets," Brigit says. "But if you won't tell her, I don't think it's going too well. Something not right about the sex. Ian's a bit off, I think."

Aussies, I mouth. Go right off.

But I liked hearing Nuala had boy trouble, depleted and wrecked as I was. I couldn't pretend I wasn't jealous of what Nuala got up to. I did most of my flirting, or what I thought was flirting, with Brigit. Brigit saw it that way too. She played along that we'd play together a bit as soon as I could get it up again. It helped moot the question of my survival; it assumed life. But she knew I had a feeling for Nuala. She was a woman and understood these things easily.

NUALA'S JUST A SCRAP OF A GIRL with a scrap of a dog and some trouble finding and keeping boyfriends. She probably has her share of neurotic fits, though she's good at keeping them to herself.

I know she's pretty tough; she managed to get herself here from Ireland, settle in New York City, which gave me a hard time when I first came up from Baltimore. The size and speed and aggression and competition that make this city almost undid me. She handled it. She works hard, very hard. People die on her all the time; it isn't a cheering profession. I see this scrap of a girl—she's cute with big eyes—and I wish I could make her a world less sad. That's not obsessive or neurotic, is it? That trip to Venice was just a dream; anything can happen in dreams. I'd apologize to Nuala if she knew about that dream. I'd be embarrassed for having had it. Unless of course she'd liked it. Then I'd be a happy man.

The hospital psychiatrist would have a good time with this one. Right, she'd say. Easy. Attachment by a patient to the caregiver who looks after him. Transference. Regularly happens in therapy. He'll forget about her within two weeks after he's discharged. Even if they go out, it'll only take one date to show them both all it was. But nurses seldom get to that point anyway. The way they see the patients doesn't really encourage very much attachment.

There are crushes sometimes, it's true. But we know how to deal with them.

CLARE HAD BROUGHT ME a little Aiwa boom box when I first came to the hospital. She's been absent for a while, but now she's shown up with a gift, something she made especially for me. I want to think it's something she's done from guilt, but I can't muster hard feelings against the only person in the world I've trusted absolutely, who has been such a friend, such a life-saver, just because she needs time to get on with her own life. She has no reason to feel guilt; she's done more than any friend could be asked. Then I congratulate myself for being so gener-ous in spirit and wonder how much is me and how much is the fentanyl.

She arrives on her lunch hour one blustery day, looking ador-able in one of her Chanelesque suits that she finds cheap at secret places in the city. She's brought two tapes for the boom box: one she's made by taping every Enya CD, and the other by scouring opera CDs for my favorite arias by sopranos. She can't stay a long time—she's got to get back to work—but I try to let her know with my eyes how pleased I am to see her and to get such a wonderful gift. She seems shy when she leaves—Clare, who's never been scared of a thing in her life. I think she must have something to tell me that she can't yet bear to say. Let her take her time. I don't care if that time never comes.

All afternoon I played Enya and later in the day let the sopra-nos break my heart. They lift me out of the bed that is breaking my body down day by day; they hold me above myself. It's hard to believe the beauty they are making is human, or meant for humans. I feel it's angelic, though I don't believe in angels.

The music kept drawing Brigit and Nuala in to have a listen. I suppose it was a nice change from the blaring TVs in most of the ward. They'd been busy with one crisis or another almost all day. Most of the rooms were occupied again. I caught glimpses of them hurrying around, carrying trays, wheeling carts. They finally come to me in the afternoon. Brigit changes my urine bag and checks the catheter in my penis. I hate it. She does it so casually, as if she were checking the oil in her car.

"So nice," Nuala says. "You like opera very much, do you?"

Only sopranos, not whole operas, I mouth to her.

"Hell, it's hard to read his lips. He mumbles too much," Brigit says. She grabs Clare's alphabet board, puts it on my chest, and takes out a pad and a ballpoint.

"So you like sopranos. The big fat ones? That makes you a little suspect in my book. Tell us, what did you do before you became our world's champion patient? Interior decoration? Florist?" Brigit asks. I point at the big letters, and Brigit writes them down as I do.

COP.

Brigit's laughing immediately. "A cop, sure. You showed up here in an Armani suit, and you still have the air of an investment banker, when you're not lying around naked showing off your prick."

Nuala smoothes my blanket. "Jesus and Mary, Brigit!"

"I just want the truth. Do you swear you are a genuine New York City cop?" Brigit asks, grabbing the catheter tube and pretending to squeeze it.

DETECTIVE LIEUTENANT BLATCHLEY. ART SQUAD.

"Art squad!" Brigit squeals and gives the tube a twist. Since I'm not in the middle of peeing it has no physical effect, but there is a psychological one. "That's a bit much to believe. They have lieutenants chase around kids who've been doing graffiti, right? You arrest kids with cans of spray paint?"

REAL ART. STOLEN PAINTINGS. SOMEBODY ALWAYS CALLS COPS.

"So you chase burglars who've lifted like million-dollar paintings from Park Avenue apartments?"

SOMETIMES. ALSO BLACK MARKET IN STOLEN ART. INSURANCE FRAUDS. COPIES. FAKES. GETS INTERESTING.

"How do you get to be a detective on the NYPD art squad? You go to the police art academy or something? They send you for training at the Louvre?" Brigit asks. She and Nuala can't stop grinning.

DID ART HISTORY AT COLUMBIA. KNEW MANET FROM MONET. LOOK SHARP IN ITALIAN SUITS. MIX OK WITH COLLECTORS. NO PRICK EVER SHOWING ON JOB.

Brigit is hysterical with laughter, Nuala is trying to tug her out of the room.

CAUGHT GUY WITH VAN DYKE DRAWING ONCE. THOUGHT HE HAD A REUBENS. DUMB FUCK. WORTH MILLIONS EITHER WAY BUT DID NOT KNOW THAT EITHER. TRYING TO SELL FOR $5,000.

Now Brigit and Nuala are suppressing their giggles like truant schoolgirls who've just been ordered to see the headmistress. Why my work is so funny to them I don't know. It's a little out of the ordinary, true, but usually the response you get from people you talk to it about for the first time isn't hysteria. I wondered if my wasted form made it hard to think that I was ever out in the world, wearing suits, taking taxis, going to art openings and cocktail parties. Then I wondered if Nuala was getting up to the same drug mischief Brigit was. I thought no, never Nuala.

THAT NIGHT, watching the clock as usual, I imagined Nuala at school with the nuns. She had a father who worked on the railways, a mother who kept the linen curtains at the windows of their cottage spotless and perfectly ironed. She had five freckled brothers. I gave her an easy adolescence, free of the sulking and pointless sadness, free of the feelings of being awkward and ugly, of being left out, of being different. I gave her a lovely loss of virginity in a hay barn with a boy who was also a virgin and was tender with her. It left her with a trust of and like for men. She did brilliantly in nursing school and was easily accepted at her hospital in New York. She had supervising nurses who were reasonable and helpful. And she found her nice one-bedroom with skylight in the five-story walk-up without too much difficulty. No one took advantage of her financially; she made it safely home when she and Brigit and other friends went down to the East Village bars and stayed too late. I kept Nuala's first years in New York securely on course.

There was little I could do about her boys, the four or five. She made sensible choices; she didn't run off with bikers or junkies or misogynist stockbrokers or reptilian lawyers. She kept away from artists and writers and musicians, with their unstable lives. None of her affairs ended badly; they just ended after a month or three or four like they do when you're in your twenties. At the fifth, I wish

I could have stepped in. It was serious. After six months, they were talking about living together.

All I know is that his name was Robbie, and he was killed, and Nuala is not yet over it. Late one day I asked Brigit with the alphabet board.

WHO WAS NUALA'S BOY?

"Robbie? An American, a nice man," Brigit said.

WHAT HAPPENED?

"He died. One day he just died."

HOW?

"I can't tell you that. That's private. That's Nuala's to say or not to say. Don't forget, you're our patient. You're not our new best friend or our brother."

LIKE TO BE. BOTH OF YOU.

"Not me." Brigit laughs. "Any plans I've got for you aren't brotherly."

I'D MADE A YOUNG LIFE for Nuala, maybe a bit smoother than it had actually been. I hoped I had done better for her than for myself. I was sensible, too. I was moderate. I traveled some and studied some. I'd been to Italy and France and England. But then I'd come back to New York and joined the force and worked and worked to make detective. For what, really? None of it was any good, except one interlude when I was very young. I had a few lovers; they usually got tired of not seeing me much. I made one great friend in Clare. After a while she was all the social life I had—going to Clare's parties, meeting Clare and her friends at clubs and restaurants. As far as work went, I never developed much of a feeling with other cops. For a few years, I made a real effort to cook myself a decent meal in my apartment each night, unless I was going out with Clare. But after a while it became too much trouble. I lived on frozen chicken pot pies and Tombstone pizzas.

It wasn't much of a world. It hadn't much of a point that I could see.

Now, at 2:45, sleeping shot useless, I lay listening to the watery monologue of The Machine. What did it mean to be dying young? Not much different from dying at sixty or seventy or eighty, I suppose, except that I got more attention from the nurses; I was unusual in their experience. People my age died of violent trauma, cancer, or AIDS. They didn't see many like me. I was a curiosity for them just as I was for the infectious disease specialists and the neurologists and the pulmonary specialists. Maybe they'd write up some little thing about me after I was dead. I'd be immortal in a medical journal: "Patient B., a previously healthy white male, smoker but no medical history, six feet tall, one hundred fifty pounds, attacked and destroyed by bacteria we grew here in our own hospital."

I WAS SOUND ASLEEP the next day when the battery of doctors arrived to announce a new course of treatment. First they watched me breathe, using stopwatches. "He's fighting The Machine. That's why we can't get everything back to normal rhythms with an active diaphragm. His body is fighting The Machine," said the doctor who appeared to be the team leader.

So they paralyzed me for five days. They gave me a miraculous drug that froze my entire body, even my eyelids and especially the major muscles of my chest and back (what was left of them). I couldn't fight anything. I was frozen. And so I breathed exactly as The Machine decided I should. They tinkered with it to get the exact timing and pressure perfect; that was important because too much pressure could rip open my fragile, wounded lungs. Plenty of antibiotic drips, of course, and the same old feeding tubes, vanilla and bitter orange.

Everyone seemed to forget that I could hear, I guess because I was still as a corpse. "Oh, sweet Jesus, he looks dead," Brigit said one day. "The Machine's the only living thing in this room. He's just a cadaver being blown up with air over and over. It makes me want to cry."

"He's alive," Nuala said. "He's still alive. He won't quit."

You have never been paralyzed for five days. You do not want to be. You want to be dead before you'll let that happen to you. When the drugs wore off I shit on myself, all over the folded sheet they'd placed under my ass for that development.

I was glad it happened when Nuala and Brigit were off duty. No doubt they'd seen it before, but I didn't want them to see me at it.

So for a while after, I breathed with The Machine. Everyone was very pleased with me, as if I'd become a star student. They decided they might not need to cut out the lower lobe of my right lung after all.

That's when the staph infection slammed into my left lung. The fever hit 103, then 104. Brain cells began to die. See what Nuala did then in my distress. She somehow made a world for me. We drove the west coast of Ireland, windshield wipers constantly going. We stood wearing Barbour jackets on green cliffs and watched green combers smash into soaring towers of white foam on the rocks below. Nuala took me to meet her parents. We had roast lamb and potatoes and soda bread for dinner. We drank ale. Her father wanted to play checkers after supper. He called me Yank. He saw that I was in love with this scrap of a girl with her wild hair and quick mind.

Of course we slept alone in separate whitewashed rooms with Christs on crosses nailed over the beds. But the sheets were crisp Irish linen, and the blankets thick natural wool. I never slept better, knowing Nuala was sleeping in the next room.

Then it was deep coma time again. Nuala wasn't on duty the day I went.

15

I'M LYING IN A BED under a canopy of mosquito netting. It's in a room walled with white-painted planks. The mattress is lumpy; everything feels damp. There's a ceiling fan above me, but the breeze it produces is dank and smells of swamp or bayou. It's night. The room is lit only by candles, tarnished silver candelabras in each corner. The light wavers with the breeze of the fan. Nuala sits in the center of the room in a big wicker chair, cooling herself with a plain bamboo fan. She's wearing only what seems to be an old-fashioned batiste peignoir. Sweat makes it cling to her flat belly and between her high breasts. She's barefoot.

I smell cooking somewhere, Cajun spices, crawfish. It's nauseating mixed with the swamp smell.

Nuala doesn't seem to notice. It's as if she can't see me behind my mosquito netting.

"I'm talking to you and you don't even hear it," she says. "Maybe that's why I feel able. It's better than a confession, because you won't punish me, will you? I won't have to say a thousand Hail Marys. You won't judge me.

"I'm sad tonight. I was walking down Greenwich Street near dusk and saw someone from behind I was sure was Robbie. My heart speeded up. I walked faster. But before I could pass him I knew it wasn't him. I know this has happened to everybody once or twice . . . the disappointment.

"Nobody in the world wants me. I had someone. I had Robbie. Oh, damn you, Robbie, get out of my life. It's time. It's been years. Yet you're still clasping me in ways I can't even describe. Whenever I get close to anyone, they sense your presence. They don't want me anymore. I'm too young to be a widow, married to your corpse. Let me go. Leave me now, can't you please?"

"Is he holding on, or are you refusing to let go of him?" I ask. I can actually hear my voice. I can talk.

"There's no way to know. We're just joined still," Nuala says. "I don't want it. It's become a nightmare. I feel he is stealing life from me, day by day. How could this good man who loved me do that to me now?"

"I don't think it's Robbie," I say. "I think it's your own fear. You frighten yourself with what you don't feel, not with what you do."

"You're lying," Nuala says. "You don't know how it is at all."

"You only say that because I've never told you about my losses, how I took them," I say. "I took them very badly, worse than you."

Suddenly I'm in a gurney being wheeled away from Nuala by a fat grinning Filipino aide. He has a high, laughing voice. "Not the place for you, oh, no. You don't want to know too much about that Nuala. She's a witch, very bad. Much better place coming up, you see," he says. He's wheeling me right down the center of a black-topped road that's empty of traffic. Into the distance, I see traffic light after traffic light, switching in sequence from green to yellow to red. The fat boy runs all the lights. No reason not to. "We're going to my place, everything the way you like it, very fine, very fine," the Filipino says. The air feels damp, but velvety. I'm breathing easily. I'm comfortable though I'm nude under a single sheet. There's a sliver of moon in the west. I see it briefly above what looks like a cluster of brightly lit motels. We're passing more and more little white clapboard houses like the one we'd come from, and now he's wheeling me through double glass doors and down around the tables of what seems to be an empty restaurant. There's a stage at one end. "My nightclub," he says. "First class, number one, no stinking Viets here. Here everything fine." He parks my gurney next to the stage. It's pale maple, like a bowling alley, but scuffed and very dirty. I hear him banging pots back in the kitchen. There are colored spotlights shining on the stage, red and yellow and orange. There's purple velvet carpet underneath me on the floor.

The fat Filipino with a face perfectly round as a ball comes out carrying a woven rattan tray, and on it are various medical instruments. "Ah, you are thinking, here are the things I like. Don't you worry. We're very well trained. We go to school long, long time to come work here."

He has pimples on his face, one near his nose that seems ready to burst. But his forearms are smooth, perfectly hairless and poreless; his hands look strong and clean. He pulls the sheet off me. I see I am strapped to this gurney. He wraps a rubber band around my right bicep and jabs a needle into a vein in my forearm. He doesn't slip it in painlessly like Nuala and Brigit; he jams it in, and it hurts like hell. Then he does the same on my left arm and just lets it dangle there. He has four or five small pediatric hypodermics in his hands now. He injects me in the belly with one, in the side of my neck with another, in my thighs with the rest. The last he injects in my eyebrow. Then he takes a metal clamp, the kind they use to close off your arteries during surgery, and clamps the middle of my penis. He inserts a long glass tube in my penis and removes the clamp. Instead of more tubing, he puts a balloon over the end of the tube. Every move he makes pinches, stings, or burns.

"Stop it, stop it," I shout. "There's no need for this."

"No, no, everything just the way you like it," he says, laughing his high, girlish laugh. "You need it like this."

"God, somebody!" I shout. "I can't stand it."

"Now, no shoutings, if you please," he says, looking pouty. "Everything just the way you like it now. Everything perfect."

Then he leaves, fat in the white coat that makes him look like a busboy. The red and green and orange lights begin to go on and off with a rhythm I can't catch. There seems to be one yellow spotlight shining steadily. I can't see into the darkened restaurant, but I have the sense that couples are walking lightly over the purple velvet carpeting, taking their places at reserved tables.

I close my eyes against the yellow spotlight and see Nuala walking back and forth in our white-planked room, twisting and untwisting a piece of her peignoir. She's whispering to Robbie: "Bastard. How could you leave me like that and haunt me like this?"

She's still barefoot; the soles of her feet are getting black from the dirty plank floor. Then she's singing an Irish song in a sweet tuneless voice: "I would I were on yonder hill, and there I'd sit and cry my fill. . . ." Her voice is huskier than when she speaks.

PURE BLACKNESS, pure silence.

Then all at once I'm back. My eyes pop open. Nothing has changed that I can see. Things are in their proper places; the smells are the familiar ICU smells. Enya's on the tape player. Brigit and Nuala are standing by my bed. They look startled. I'm not in the usual daze. I'm present, acute, energized, and they see this. I think about what I ought to say. Quickly I decide to tell Nuala she was with me, that we talked. I motion for my board. I point faster than I've ever managed. "Just a dream," Nuala says, after Brigit writes down the letters.

YOU KNOW ITS NO DREAM. WE ARE ALL OVER THERE, A DIFFER-
ENT DIMENSION.

"No, we monitor the brain waves, and it's similar to being
asleep," Nuala says. "Anyway, everybody's in everybody else's
dreams. I even dreamt of you not long ago."

DOING WHAT?

"None of your business."

YOU SPOKE TO ME. ASKED ROBBIE TO SET YOU FREE.

"I never did," Nuala said, paling. "How could you know that?
There is no Robbie!" She burst into tears and ran from the room.

"Oh, great," said Brigit. "That's the last time I spell out your
thoughts for you. What's all this crap you think up when you're
in your comas? While you were out, we've been over at the Bells.
I left with Bob, and Nuala left alone. No Ian. But you didn't
know anything about that, did you? So why scare her with the
crap you make up? Now she'll think I told you about Robbie, and
you know damn well the little I said was supposed to stay between you and me. I ought to pop you one on the jaw," Brigit
said.

She threw down my alphabet board, breaking off one of the
corners, and followed Nuala into the nurses' room.

The broken corner of my board almost made me cry. I have
so little already, I thought. Clare made that for me. Then I got
a grip and smothered my self-pity with anger at the whole wide
world.

16

I HEAR THEM TALKING ABOUT ME. And I hear other things: wet whistling, a dull repetitive thud, but also the soft Irish voices. Lilting, yes, there's a reason for that good word. When they speak to each other there's the Irish lilt, except maybe among those from the rough parts of Belfast. Belfast voices are harsh, like the lives there. These are musical. I don't want to open my eyes for fear of scaring them away. I have the ridiculous notion they're like fairies with transparent wings who'd flee from my sight instantly.

The IV in my right inner wrist is stinging constantly now. It needs to be changed. It's so odd to have things dripping into your veins, hour after hour, never stopping. You don't feel the liquid entering you, there must be some counterpressure that makes the mixing of the medicine and your blood unnoticeable physically. But you know something foreign is entering you. You feel invaded.

It can't be very late, not much after midnight. I got my sleeping dose around 11:00. When it works, as it seems to have tonight, I'm gone in an hour or so. I open my right eye a crack; the clock says 12:30. I can see dim lights outside my room in the ward, but my room is dark except for the red and blue and green pinlights in my life-support equipment. Would I pull the plug, if I could reach it? Would I have that kind of courage? I doubt it.

I can see Nuala and Brigit standing just inside my door. They're not in uniform; they're in their boy clothes: short skirts, sexy little shoes. Do they stop in on their way home from the Bells of Hell just on the impulse to check on their prize patient? They trust Patricia and Susan and the night shift, but probably sometimes they like to see for themselves, especially since they know I don't always sleep.

"How can he not be HIV?" Brigit says in a low voice. They think I'm asleep and have decided they don't want to wake me up.

"You know he was clean on the tests. Maybe he just had a bum immune system, too much stress, too much work, and the worst chicken pox anybody's ever seen."

"Sweet Mary! And the rottenest luck. It ate him alive."

"He makes me think of Robbie," Nuala says. "Brigit, why did you tell him?"

"I never did, I swear to Jesus."

"He knew the name, Brigit."

"Probably from you. You talk to him a lot more than you realize. And he's nothing like Robbie."

"I know. It's just the idea of someone getting struck down so young, so suddenly. It breaks my heart."

"Do you think he was good-looking?"

"Couldn't tell with the pox all over him. But his photo sure looks good. He's lucky he doesn't have more scars. If he had twenty or thirty more pounds on him, he'd be sort of pretty for a man his age. A little scary, maybe. But you'd look twice if he smiled at you at the Bells."

"I look twice at everyone who smiles at me," Brigit said. "Old Dublin habit, where, my darling, as you know, the good men are few and far between."

"At least there were some. Christ, you should have seen it around Bantry."

"Greasy oil riggers, grab your tits by way of saying hello. I know the type. Black grime under their fingernails."

Nuala shook her head.

They were quiet for a minute.

"You're going to kill yourself, Brigit," Nuala said suddenly. "You've got to stop."

"Ah, it's under control. It's just a pediatric hypo every now and then. Where's the harm? It gets me through the days," Brigit said.

"We've all got days to get through. The same blood, vomit, agony, and fear. You know what I go through every time this one here goes under? I feel like shit."

"Try the fentanyl. It saves you. It makes you better at your work."

"Bullshit. It's fooling you. It just makes you numb for a couple hours, 'til you've got to shoot again," Nuala said.

"Yeah, like it makes him numb," Brigit said.

"He needs it. He's critical, for God's sake. There's nothing wrong with you."

"Just my fucked-up life. I can't face the pain on the faces of these people anymore. I want to run away every time the boys with the body bags come by. I go to bed with nice boys who wake up with bad breath and want more fentanyl, or anything they can get. They can't even imagine their own mortality. They're alive because they never, ever think of death. I'm scared of it every single waking moment, day in, day out."

"Some sad story. We've all got some sad story. But we get on with things. Please, Brigit, you've got to stop. If it doesn't get you, the supervisors will. Your career will be over."

"I could care less," Brigit said. "I don't think I can take it much longer anyway. I'd almost rather be a bartender."

I hear rubbery footsteps outside my room. "Hey, Patricia," Brigit says. "How's our old man tonight?"

"Tough as ever. Signs were all good when we put him to sleep."

"When's this ordeal going to be over?" Nuala asks, though she knows Patricia has no more idea than she.

"When it's time," Patricia says. "Just like for everybody else."

I'M AWAKE FOR A LONG WHILE after they've gone. To pass the time, I decide to make something for Nuala. A box like

Joseph Cornell used to make in his basement. I use an old orange crate with colorful labels of Indians stuck on the sides. And for the inside, I have my choice of everything in the universe. The first thing I attach, near the top of the box, is a small but very sharp photo of a full moon, one in which you can clearly see the smooth dark lava flows and the upthrust peaks and the dusty depths of craters. It has that silvery quality, not just rocky gray but silvery. In one corner I put a tiny old photograph of me, age two, in a short-sleeved white shirt and knit tie that is much too large. My hair is cut so close to my head that you can see the funny little cowlick I still have right at the edge of my forehead. You can see I've been crying; probably I was afraid of the photographer. But in this shot, though the tears are glistening, I am looking up and off to the left, presumably where my mother must have been standing, and I have a tentative but hopeful smile. I add a key holder made of colorful Indian beads I must have made at day camp one summer, and my junior varsity football letter, in navy and orange. I put in a crumpled faded ticket to a tiny circus I once went to in the Italian Alps, and a sepia postcard of *Susanna and the Elders* I bought in a street market in Florence. Finally I added the key to my old black Jaguar.

Then I realized my box was a total failure—nothing but a crowd of relics from my own life, nothing to do with Nuala, nothing to say to her. It wasn't for her at all; it was for me. That was the genius of Cornell; his worlds spoke to everyone without ever leaving the basement of his mother's house in Queens. Everything he did came directly from his soul, not what he saw of the world.

I WAS STILL contemplating my failure when the cold sponge-bath women came in to torment me. The pain shoots through my body as they roll me over and back. But it feels good to be shaved, and I'm drifting back into a pleasant warm doze when Cindy shows up with another therapist I've never met. Her name is Cindy too, and she's going to work on my claw. She heats a sheet of matte white plastic in a pan of hot water while she has a look at my wrist. She can tell by my face that straightening it is agonizing. But she persists. "We've got to get it back to a normal position. That's what the brace is going to do," she says.

When the plastic is soft enough to be workable, she takes it out of the water, gets the other Cindy to straighten my wrist, and molds it over my elbow to just where my fingers meet my palm. The warmth of the plastic is soothing, but it doesn't do anything for the pain. When the plastic has stiffened, she attaches a sort of raised bridge of metal that looks like a piece of stainless steel coat hanger. Then she loops thick rubber bands around the metal bridge and hooks them over my fingers. She orders me to bend my fingers. I can, but the rubber strips immediately straighten them when I give up trying.

"Perfect," says the new Cindy. "It's called a cantilever brace. Wear this for a month and your wrist drop will be fixed." It hurts like hell. "You'll just have to take the pain for a few days. It'll fade."

"He's a tough guy; he likes a little pain," the real Cindy says. "He's always trying to wrestle with me even though he knows I could put his ass on the floor just like that."

Your time will come, I mouth at Cindy, and she laughs. I can't understand how these medical people can keep any sense of humor, dealing with what they do every day.

Nuala, Brigit, Patricia, and everyone else who visits my room that day have a good, long look at my new brace. "Cool," Brigit says when she sees me bend my fingers. I'm supposed to practice bending them as often as I can.

Clare comes that night just after dinner. She's looking chic as usual, obviously on her way out somewhere, Au Bar or the Royalton. She gives me a kiss on the cheek, then hands me my alphabet board and pulls a notebook from her purse. I get the feeling this is going to be serious. I haven't seen her in a week or so.

"You look good. You've gained some weight? I see they're finally fixing your wrist."

I smile and flex my fingers at her.

"I haven't been coming, I know. I feel like a weakling but I can't stand it here. Every time I come, I'm haunted for days," she says.

SURE, I point.

"It isn't you. I think about you all the time. But it hurts my heart to see you like this. Does that make sense?"

YEAH. IT SCARES YOU.

"God, it's worse than that. I feel like your damn illness has stolen you from me."

CHICKENSHIT, I point.

"I can't help it. I cry myself to sleep. I feel lost. During the day, I wonder what you're doing like I used to before all this, and then I remember where you are and what's happening to you and I cry."

YOU CRY? WHAT YOU THINK I DO? I was raging inside.

"But my life has a huge hole in it."

LEAST YOU GOT LIFE. FILL IT.

"Now, I'm a coward, trying for your sympathy like this. I have filled it. I've got a lover, a real one. It almost makes up for everything."

Clare and I hadn't been lovers. We'd been better, like brother and sister. I was always the one with lovers on the side. Yet this was harder than I'd imagined.

HAPPY FOR YOU. GLAD YOU TOLD ME. No way to be sarcastic with an alphabet board.

"Can you mean that? I didn't dare hope you'd understand. I came here expecting to hurt you so badly. I put it off and off and off, because I couldn't bear the idea."

STILL FRIENDS?

"Of course. I couldn't ever abandon you. I love you. It's just that coming here is so hard."

GET THE FUCK OUT.

She's crying, sitting perfectly still but with tears, which she doesn't bother to wipe away, coursing down her cheeks. Her careful makeup is being ruined. The part of me that isn't crushed and frightened and furious suddenly feels bold.

ONE CONDITION. YOU AND YOUR MAN THROW BIG PARTY WITH

TONS OF PRETTY YOUNG GIRLS FOR ME AFTER I GET OUT. And I won't fucking show up.

"The best party you ever saw," Clare says, rising from her chair and coming to kiss me. She takes my left hand and kisses each fingertip. "Love you always," she says, and turns to go. She almost bumps into Nuala.

"Hey, Clare, been a while." It sounds arch and strange coming from her.

"Yes, I've been bad," Clare says. "Got to run. Good-bye."

Nuala's big green eyes hardly leave mine while she's taking my temperature. She's dying to know what just went on. I'm stone-faced: She'll never find out from me. 98.6! Perfect.

Fuck Clare. I feel, beyond abandonment, a great relief. My world is getting simpler and simpler. Pretty soon it'll be so minimalist I'll glide through it—or out of it—as smoothly as if I were Teflon-coated. Or as if I were a ghost. I give Nuala my best grin, thinking of worlds I might make for her, worlds she'd love without even knowing where they came from.

"Odd sense of humor you have, Mr. Blatchley," Nuala says. "That girl was in tears over you, and you dare smile at me like that."

You don't understand, I mouth. Been dumped. Won't ever see her again. Bet on it.

Then it was Nuala's eyes that filled with tears.

17

NEXT DAY NUALA COMES into my room, sits down, and slips off her shoes. The ICU hasn't any new customers just now. She'd like to relax in silence. I gesture for my alphabet board. She's reluctant, but brings it over, and takes a pad and pencil to write.

BANTRY?

"You sneaky sod. Eavesdropping like any dirty old man. Shame on you."

WHAT ABOUT BANTRY?

"Not Bantry at all. A little rathole at the head of Bantry Bay called Glengarriff—tawdry was the way the guidebooks described it when they were being charitable. Too many pubs and loose women, everything run-down and shabby. My da worked down the bay on Whiddy Island, at the big oil terminal. The workers used to come up Glengarriff for their pints in the evening. Best for a girl not to be on the streets at pub closing time.

"I always thought it funny that Bantry House, what everyone said was the most beautiful property in all Ireland, was a hop and skip from that ugly oil terminal. Funny too when they shut down the terminal and put my da on the dole for the rest of his life. Lots of laughs for lots of people."

YOUR MA AND DA NOW?

"Writing sometimes, sometimes asking for a little money. The begging ones always come from Da, not my mother. He always writes about how they sacrificed so I could go to school with the nuns and get a good education, and how now they find themselves in their lonely old age just a bit short of the ready, and wouldn't a few dollars be welcome."

SO YOU WERE WHITE-SOCK VIRGIN WHEN YOU WENT UP TO DUBLIN MET BRIGIT.

"Never was, mister. And none of your business in particular, the raw life you've led. Brigit just has a mouth on her bigger than fits her face."

MUST HAVE GOT NEW IDEA OF TAWDRY FIRST TIME YOU SAW EAST VILLAGE?

"Why do you think I'm such an innocent? Because I've got a kid's face? I bet I've seen more of real life than you. I'm sure I've seen more death. What those children are playing at in the East Village is nothing but a traveling minstrel show, with occasional casualties. We get some in here. They are, each and every one, not tough at all. They're scared shitless because they got hurt and it's finally dawned on them what the next step could be."

TOUGH ATTITUDE.

"Don't patronize me, Mr. Art Cop. Go arrest Egon Schiele for drawing little girls playing with their pussies."

NUALA!

"Sometimes it's hard not to get angry at you, especially because of what you want to know. If we were friends outside this place, you'd get to know everything you wanted in the natural way friendships grow. It's weird here."

WEIRD, BECAUSE SOMETIMES I DON'T CONNECT YOU WITH THIS PLACE AT ALL.

"What do you mean?"

SOMETIMES FEELS WE MET OUT IN WORLD AND THAT'S WHERE WE ARE. TALKING, WALKING, FLIRTING FOR THE FUN EVEN IF YOU AREN'T INTERESTED. REAL LIFE, UNDERSTAND.

"No, I don't see it much like that at all. To me it feels like you're a patient, but you're a long-term patient I've gotten to be fond of. Usually we turn 'em around pretty quickly up here."

ANYWAY YOU'VE GIVEN ME SENSE OF LIFE OUTSIDE MACHINES AND TUBES. THANK YOU. NEVER MEAN TO OFFEND.

"You don't. You just upset me sometimes."

IF I'M BAD DO WHAT CINDY THREATENS.

"What's that?"

YANK CATHETER OUT HARD AS SHE CAN.

Nuala started laughing. "Cindy's just the one to do it too, especially if you keep making her self-conscious about her breasts."

NEVER DO THAT.

"You always do. You have very expressive eyes."

"Oh, and next you'll be telling him how handsome his chis-eled features are, like a younger Clint Eastwood, and how Cindy's nipples always push out against her sweatshirt when she gets near him." Brigit walked in, bright-eyed and cheerful. "You'll be saying all those hideous scars on his chest just make him look rugged and manly."

"I think maybe it's you that takes tips from Miss Marriage. 'Oh, yes, now we are having fine therapy, just you wait one jiffy,' " Nuala mimics.

I start to laugh so hard I begin to choke. Brigit quickly yanks off my blue tube and sticks a suction so deep into the hole I feel I'm going to vomit my lungs up. The light hissing of the suction quickly turns into a slow, thick slurping sound, and the tube is filled with dark green phlegm streaked with white and a few threads of red. It's my fault. I've been taught now how to suction myself a few times a day, but I rarely do it until the breathing gets difficult.

"If you were pure Irish I'd say you were one dumb Mick. You probably haven't suctioned in five or six hours. Look at this disgusting mess," she says, holding the tube in front of my face.

Later that evening when Nuala is leaving, she stops by my room. "I'll tell you some things for free, since you're so inter-ested. Living in Ireland is like living at the bottom of a damp, old well. The stone walls are covered completely with a slimy moss that smells of ancient decay, so you've no chance in hell of climbing out. You're stuck in there with all the other frogs and newts. But through the round opening overhead, you can see people passing by, doing things, free in the open air. You can see sunshine and massing clouds. You can see a world moving and living life out of the dank darkness. You've no way to join them unless somebody takes pity on you and throws you down a rope.

"Nursing was my rope. It's the hardest work—I never would have chosen it—but given a choice between that and staying in the well, it was a gift from the blessed Jesus."

Naturally, I think, someone tells you something like that and you begin to consider your own gifts from blessed Jesus or Yaweh or Allah or whoever has your attention. You can make lists, good versus bad, and decide if you've gotten a fair deal. Who's deciding what's "fair" doesn't much matter when you're in that mood. So you say thanks for the job you've still got, for the insurance that's paying your bills, that you've gotten this far without being killed, and that you're not a vegetable yet. The rest of it—that you're not rich, that you haven't found the love of your life and married her, that you don't have the body and constitution of a twenty-five-year-old anymore, that you've learned about the abridgement of hope, that you've seen now how the speed of life accelerates completely out of your control, that nothing you plan or plot can overcome destiny—may seem out of balance but it isn't really, because none of it was picked for you as a special affliction. It's just the carrying of life, which we are all strong enough to bear until the day our strength fails.

Nuala is a strong one, I can tell. The strong ones usually don't

have extravagant hopes. That's not to say they're too easily satis-
fied; it is to say they're content if they get what they work for.
They don't expect to win the lottery. They don't feel entitled to
anything.

SO INSTEAD OF working on a world that night, I make an adven-
ture that would show Nuala a world she hasn't seen (having been
only between Bantry and Dublin and New York City). We don't
have to worry about the irritations of travel—visas, shots, layovers.

It's me doing this after all, my drugged, disorderly mind. It's
just me taking my good friend Nuala for a trip.

There are no dank wells, no newts and frogs in Arizona. We
are staying in a cabin on a ranch, and every day at dawn we ride
beautifully trained quarterhorses up into the dry, yellow-grass hills
that were Cochise's stronghold in the days of the Apaches. From
the tops you can see fifty miles across an absolutely flat desert valley
to 10,000-foot mountains where, as you climb higher and higher,
you enter forests of huge pines filled with deer. The sun's almost
too much for Nuala; she wears a hat and sunglasses, and plenty of
sunscreen, but still her skin reddens; her hair gets more coppery. I
teach her to shoot a Colt. She likes the feel and the bang of it but
can't hit a thing she aims at.

Ah, then there are the linen sheets, of course, in room 323 at
the Villa d'Este, with the little iron balcony overlooking the lake.
There are two beds; I'm not trying to seduce her. I would like,

eventually, for her to ask me, but that is not the point either. We're wearing the big white terry-cloth robes when the waiter brings caffe latte and blood orange juice and brioche to our balcony. Nuala is luxuriating. Later we'll lie around the pool, which floats in the deep blue of Lake Como. Nuala will wear a dark green one-piece racing suit. And I've never seen her in anything so revealing. Each night she puts on her flannel pajamas in the bathroom. Her shoulders are broader than her hips, like a real swimmer. Even the tight elastic doesn't cut into her firm thighs. There's no fat on her.

We go to Bologna to eat. Every night a different restaurant until we have tried every specialty of the region and persuaded every sommelier to produce an unlabeled bottle of local wine he reserves for his regular customers.

We drive north in the big new Citroen I've rented and climb the Drei Zinnen. It's the highest mountain in the Dolomite Alps. We are on top of the world. I'm transformed. I've never breathed more easily in my life, the absolutely clean air of 4,000 meters. We can see for a hundred miles. And that night we lie between the perfectly ironed linen sheets of the Hotel de la Poste, in separate beds.

All night the globe revolves for Nuala and me. We swim in the Celebes Sea; we snorkel in the Coral Sea; we walk along the Bund in Shanghai; we visit the Zambezi Falls and the crocodiles of Lake Victoria. We spend a night deliberately marooned alone on an islet of the Seychelles, watching the Southern Cross wheel in its course.

And when we return to New York, I throw a big party at my loft. We have so many friends we can't count them. They all treat us as a couple even though we're not.

NUALA LOOKS AT ME so oddly the next morning when she comes to take my temperature. Her green eyes are searching mine. "Where were you last night, James?" she asks. "Were you traveling the world with a girl you scarcely know, being sweet, trying to turn her head? Did you take her to places she only knows from maps?"

Don't remember, I mouth. Just normal dreams, I think.

"No, not normal. I was the girl, James. It was clear as could be. The Dolomites, the Southern Cross, shooting a Colt. I could smell the sweaty horses. What cause would I have to dream of such things?

"I told Brigit," Nuala continues, bending over me. She must have used chamomile shampoo this morning. I close my eyes. "Brigit said the worst isn't the trespass, but that you never even laid a hand on me. Typical Brigit."

Just dreams, I mouth. Who can explain? Sometimes people meet there.

"Brigit said you can't do it. You can't just go strolling through someone else's dreams, take control, and expect to get away with it. She said to tell you it's like breaking and entering; that's something you'd know about.

"Actually it was rather a lovely dream. You were in it. We traveled to wonderful places." Nuala smiles.

I know, I mouth. You like Villa d'Este best.

"You're just guessing now, mister," Nuala says. "If you were really there, you'd know what sort of swim costume I was wearing."

I mouth, Green tank.

Nuala looks a little moonstruck, but says, "It's all I ever wear. Brigit could tell you that. You two are up to no good."

I mouth, We aren't. She didn't say your horse was named Goose, either.

"Goose." Nuala pales.

I WAS AS SHOCKED as she seemed to be. Was something being given to my mind in exchange for what had been killed? How could such a connection be made? I wanted so much to talk to Nuala. I hoped she'd come to me that night.

Instead at midnight I was woken by two black orderlies who lifted me onto a gurney and tried to set a speed record down endless corridors to a room very much like the CAT-scan room. This time it's an MRI, another claustrophobic, shiny steel tube that made diabolical noises, another Machine. "We're looking for inflammation of the spinal cord," the doctor conducting the scan said. "We're trying to find out why your diaphragm only works intermittently. That's the key to getting you off The Machine and out of here. Or at least into rehab."

Cindy runs rehab, I mouthed.

"Yeah, it's little Cindy. She'll teach you to walk and do every-thing again. She's got tits like the most squeezable lemons you've ever seen." He laughed. "You can look right down her sweatshirt you know, the necks are always baggy."

18

BRIGIT SEES BOB almost every night. But she's not in love; none of the signs are there. It's just great sex, the kind that comes along every once in a while. Until one day the hormones stop zinging and you're left looking at each other, wondering what happened.

I don't hear much of Ian. Never did from Nuala, and now seldom even from Brigit. But Nuala has taken to dropping by my room more often at the end of the day to have a chat. She calls it that anyway. She won't use the alphabet board with me, so it's more of a monologue. I feel like she's gone a long time with no one to really listen to her. She likes to think I believe she's hard-bitten—her dad on the dole in a rotten ex-oil town—but she gives herself away as naively as a child. Or maybe that's the only way she can face saying what she says.

There was a curragh after all. There was an old man who loved her company and taught her what he knew.

"Nearly every soft day after school, I'd run to my grandda's house, hoping he'd feel like a sail. He seldom let me down, though his hands were so arthritic he could barely grasp the oars. We'd go out in his old curragh, one of the last in Bantry, and fish. He said he knew all the secret spots from the old days, but we never caught anything worth taking home for supper. I never cared. It was enough that he wanted to show me things, that he'd let me row when we weren't in tricky waters even though I was only eight or ten.

"When I had the oars, he stuffed his old briar pipe with tobacco he'd gathered from cigarette butts around the town and puff away. It did have a nicer smell than pipe tobacco. I tried it a few times. It made me feel dizzy, but in such a nice way I wanted more.

"I'd handle the boat, and Grandda would watch the weather. He'd explain the difference between mare's tails and herringbones, and how high cumulus boded different from cirrus, and how to smell a storm. You could really feel it in your sinuses if you paid attention. Like a sort of built-in barometer.

"The best was the spring when I was twelve. We repainted the curragh. He let me choose the colors. I picked a lovely royal blue for the hull, a lime green for the trim, and brilliant orange for the oars. People came along to watch us work; they'd never seen a curragh like that and probably haven't since.

"Once when he was at the pub, I sneaked down and painted

'Blue Johnny' on the bow as a name. His name was Johnny. When he first saw it he looked cross; he muttered about it being bad luck to sail a boat named after yourself. But then he grinned and gave me a hug and wanted to cast off right away, before the paint was dry.

"Why do I tell you these things? They're the sweetnesses of my life. It seems a shame never to share them with someone who might understand what Blue Johnny could mean to a green girl. Here, I suppose, all the rich girls have their horses. Well, I had my curragh, and my grandda to go with it, more's the better. And I'm thinking after all these weeks together that you're a man who'd understand.

"If it bothers you, I'll stop. But I do say it's a pleasure for me to tell the tales. It makes them more real to me, in a way."

I had nothing so beautiful in my own world to share. I reached out with my braced left hand. She took it and gently straightened the fingers, one by one. As soon as one straightened the other curled shut, but Nuala kept at it finger after finger, silent and kind and soft.

"At first I didn't want to get to know you at all. I could tell you noticed I was cold, but then you understood it was the nature of the job. Our hearts would be broken if we got fond of people in the ICU. You saw that.

"But now, mister, I wish you could tell your stories too. Not by alphabet board. That's not really talking. I want to hear your words, the tone of your voice. I want to see the way your face moves. I want to hear about your curragh . . .

"Bless that blue tube for saving your life, and curse it too for cutting you off from me," Nuala said.

NUALA WAS VERY SHY the next day. Strictly professional. Brigit noticed of course but ignored it. Brigit kept teasing me, the way she always did. I'd try to catch Nuala's eyes, but they'd elude mine, then flick back for just a glimpse. It felt a little like young love. That's the way I remember it—the approach, then the withdrawn next meeting. But it wasn't. Nuala wouldn't let it happen. I have no idea what she wants. But I feel I want to be closer. I want to be her closest brother, full of pride and love. I'd give her anything, just for a smile, for a long look from those eyes. Her eyes refused. Disappointment must have shown on my face.

"You know," Brigit said, "I bet you're the type that goes moony over Yeats." Where she got her skill in reading moods I'll never know. "You seem sad-hearted today, like someone who was watching the wild swans and stumbled into the drink."

Fuck that. If I wasn't where I was and how I was, would I have given Nuala a second look? Wouldn't she be as anonymous as a sparrow out in the world? I'm trying hard to convince myself of something here, to save myself from something hopeless. I conclude it's Brigit who reads too much Yeats. Too heady for her, all that murmuring a little sadly how love fled and hid his head among a cloud of stars. The time for all that died long before we were born.

We don't understand romantic love anymore. It cripples you to believe in it. Yet I think Brigit does, and she behaves as oppositely as she can.

I think Brigit is the type who really wants to be married and have a lot of babies. She'll never admit it. I also think she's the kind of girl who has trouble every morning finding a pair of stockings without runs. I think she kicks her dirty underwear under the bed every night and never washes any until the day comes she has to go naked under her uniform. The drain in her bathtub is clogged with hair, and she nicks her legs using old plastic razors. I think she buys expensive shampoo and conditioner and always forgets to put the tops back on. Brigit, I think, worries about her bikini line in the summer. She does crunches every morning starting in February to get her stomach flat for summer.

These are all the strange mysteries of women that make me care for them so. Sure.

Brigit has me figured out even better than I have her, I think. She knows I've been something of a parasite on Clare. That I'm lonely and afraid of being alone. That I'm a womanizer because of that. But I resent it when a perfectly lovely girl strews her things around my loft or doesn't replace the top on the toothpaste tube. She believes I could never be faithful to one woman for long. She thinks I'm after Nuala because I can smell she's wounded, even though I'm half-dead.

"You're a hound," Brigit says. "You were bred to hunt. If you weren't sick, you'd have already tried to do Nuala, Susan, even me, just for sport. In Ireland, greyhounds chase rabbits. Born a dog, die a dog. But there're no rabbits here for you.

"Anyway, you're not dying on us. You'll see."

THAT'S ALL BETWEEN FEVERS, of course. When I'm really sick the level of banter goes way down. I can tell how serious I am by the way Brigit talks and the way Nuala looks. But also by the number of visits by the infectious disease specialist, the pulmonary expert, and the surgeon who can't wait to slip in and cut out my lower right lung. I picture him holding it in his gloved hand like a trophy. He says it's necrotic, the source of all my troubles, and must be eliminated. "Let's try another lung draining," the pulmonary man always says, and so far he has kept the scalpel from me.

19

SOME DAYS I DON'T HURT MUCH, or feel strange in my mind. They're the good days; they last forever. I wish to God they wouldn't.

It's better to have something to fight against. It passes the time between sleep and sleep.

On the good days, there's a limit to how many of your own memories you can call up without succumbing to a nostalgia that almost breaks you. There's a shorter limit to how many pleasant futures you can imagine (never a strong point with me anyway) before they all seem like delusions. And there's a definite limit to how long you can divert yourself—counting drops of various colored IVs, watching rhythms of red and green lights, staring at the damn big clock that secretly slips backward in time.

Sometimes on clear days I try to think about art, sort of keeping my hand in my trade. Not particular paintings, not schools or techniques, not my own past cases. But about the lives artists led. I wonder how Schiele felt at twenty-eight, his lungs rotten with pneumonia the way mine have been. Were there last regrets as he felt life slipping away from him (only three days after the death of his pretty young wife from the Spanish flu)? You do feel it slipping, you know. It's not just an expression.

But I think most often of poor Vincent. I feel on a first-name basis, even though I've only seen a half-dozen works in the flesh, read one biography. And I've seen that movie about him they made in the '50s with Kirk Douglas. I think of Vincent all by himself in a bright blue rowboat, in a river with almost no current, so he doesn't need an anchor. He stops where he pleases, sets up his easel, and paints. The river barely moves, but he drifts enough so that he must paint in a hurry, slathering on the pigments quickly and thickly before he loses his perspective. He never paints the river, only the workers in the fields nearby, the distant church towers, the flat fecund landscape of . . . I don't know where. Flanders in the summer? He always starts with yellow; it cheers him to lay it on thick. The darker colors come later, the shadows, the haunting tones. Later, when he's ready for the reality of what he's making. He works hard all day, stopping only to sip water from a wicker-covered bottle from time to time. When the light fades, he rows himself someway back up the river. Sometimes he stops at my rickety dock and comes into my hut. We eat bowls of lamb stew and drink rough red local wine. Sometimes Nuala drops in, wearing long, full peasant skirts and heavy wooden shoes. Nuala again, always Nuala. Maybe we are in Flanders. She pulls up a chair to my cracked walnut table and watches us eat and drink.

Otherwise, Vincent never leaves the river. It's as good as his own. Nobody cares at all what he does out there. Not a soul is interested. The peasants think he's a mental case and are polite to him, waving their straw hats. Nuala gives him a piece of bread stuffed with leftover stew for his lunch tomorrow. He likes to sleep in his boat, to catch the new light at dawn. He sulks under a tarpaulin and smokes his pipe when it rains.

"Vincent, my friend," I say. "You've got to leave here. You've got to take your work somewhere where people can see it. At least send it to a dealer if you won't go yourself."

"I send it to my brother. He's a dealer," Vincent says. "He tries very hard, but no one is interested. No one at all."

"Then why go on? Doesn't every artist need an audience? Doesn't every work of art need to be seen?"

"Oh, mine's seen all right," he says, tapping his temple and lighting his enormous pipe. His face disappears behind a nimbus of blue smoke. "And in addition to me, you see and sometimes Nuala and once in a while a farmer. I showed one the other day to a man who'd broken his back with a scythe all day. 'Goddamn crows,' he said. 'You got those thieving bastards just right. The color of your hay's a little off, though.' "

"But Vincent, what about a big show in someplace like Paris? Don't you want to sell, to be recognized?"

"What for? I've been to Paris. Half the time I felt I was only dreaming it, and the other half I felt like a stranger to myself. Where I go is into my pictures. I live in them, when I'm not eating your lamb stew." He chuckles. "Paris isn't real. Real's me on my boat, putting the yellow on canvas."

He puffs a huge blue cloud. "A bit of money would help, it's true. I hate asking my brother for money for paint."

My Vincent makes me want to cry. It makes me feel murderous to know that some man who will never know him like I do, never understand the yellow, paid $42 million for *Sunflowers*. Just an investment, just for prestige. It makes me want to shoot that man.

I want Nuala to understand this, but I've no way to tell her. She'd think I was mad if she knew about her visits to my shack in Flanders by a slow deep-green river to watch Vincent van Gogh eat stew. But she was becoming everything to me, like Vincent's pictures.

Even on a good day like that I'm losing my mind, I think. Something with the inflammation of my spinal cord and my brain is making all the synapses go haywire. I've never had such an imagination in my life. There are tiny sparks in my head between tiny plugs and sockets that don't quite fit snugly together. They've worked loose, somehow; the connections are dangerously tenuous.

I wonder what Vincent would have done with Nuala. He wasn't much of a portraitist (except of himself). But her colors might have inspired him. They are close to his own; his hair was more orange, but her eyes are deeper green. I try to imagine Nuala's face as Vincent would have done it. But she's too classical, too regular. Vincent would have more success with Brigit. Brigit's vitality would have made Vincent feel real. He could have done her in four colors, no more.

IT WAS AFTER A DAY like that that they told me I had reached the limit with fentanyl. I was at the very maximum dosage they thought they could use without causing permanent damage to organs like my kidneys. This was explained to me by a third-year resident who had not yet learned how to deal with patients as intelligent adults. But of course he thought anyone on the drug dosage I was on couldn't possibly be lucid. He tried to say, in the simplest way, that from now on each day they would lower the fentanyl dosage by six percent. Then, when the dosage had been cut thirty percent, they would begin to substitute with morphine, and build that up only if they had to.

They'd have to. Pretty quickly, too. The very first night I went into withdrawal, eyes rolling, limbs thrashing, sweat pouring off me, terrible headache, double vision, and a strange echoing of all sounds. The bad girls came to tie me to the bed again. I was clear enough mentally to suffer all this, and although I couldn't say what I was longing for, my body was clearly displeased.

I wondered if it would be this way for Brigit when she finally quit. Or would she be able to bring herself down more easily?

In the night they reluctantly gave me some other drug to ease the withdrawal, like methadone for a heroin addict. But I never slept a moment; they changed my bedclothes twice. And still in the morning when Nuala and Brigit arrived, they saw me trembling, black circles under my eyes and face oily with sweat. They looked at each other for a moment and went out in the hall to talk. I could see them through the big glass window. Some idiot on the night staff had left my TV on. Now it was blaring *Good Morning, America*. The talking heads were so cheerful, as if somewhere in Iowa a boy hadn't gotten both arms ripped off at the shoulder by a combine, as they reported. Or a baby hadn't been born blind and AIDS-infected two floors down from me.

"Some white-coat asshole you've never seen before tried to de-fentanyl you last night, didn't he?" Brigit said, coming back into the room.

"Six percent first cut. That's crazy at his level. It should have been two at most," Nuala said, reading the chart. She took my temperature. 102. "Not too bad, considering. God, when will these residents learn to read charts? Susan should have known better than to let him do this."

"Susan can't overrule a resident. Anyway, if it's the one I'm thinking of, he's the one she's been shtupping lately."

I felt safer now, with Nuala here. I asked for my alphabet board.

NURSES DO IT WITH DOCTORS? SHOCKED!

Brigit laughed. "We can't all be virgins like Saint Nualala. If we were, no men would study medicine and become doctors. And then where would you be?"

NURSED TO HEALTH BY ANGELS.

"You're right, we probably could," Brigit said. "Except for little things like the three-inch incisions in your throat for the trache, or slicing holes in your side."

"Oh, I could do the side holes. I might need some practice on the traches, though. Could I practice on you?" Nuala said. Something in her voice sounded serious, like she believed she could be a surgeon instead of an RN.

"No, I want to get my belly button pierced before I get into scarification," Brigit said.

"I'll only leave one small lovely scar," Nuala said. "Mr. Blatchley would trust me, I'm sure."

Then Myala came swaying into the room. Nuala smiled. "Time for some fine therapy," Myala said to me, pointedly ignoring the others. "We're cleaning out your lungs. You're not looking so well today, Mr. Handsome Fellow. These nurses mistreating you good or what? You just say so to Myala, and she have them fixed but good."

Nuala and Brigit started to walk out, Brigit swinging her ass more than necessary.

"That's right, better you leave us to get on with it," Myala said. Her eyes seemed excessively kohled this morning, and her nose diamond twinkled.

So I breathe her smoke while Myala keeps looking between me and my photo, as if she has some lingering doubts we are the same man.

I'M CRAVING SOMETHING. My body feels hollow. It's demanding to be fed. Actual food. Something other than what goes down the tube. And I need my dope. This day is much too long already and it's only just started. I can't sleep. After a while, I smell coffee brewing in the nurses' station. My mouth is so dry I'd drink anything liquid, but it's all forbidden. I want out of this present.

When Brigit comes in again I ask her to bring me my three art books. I start to study the van Gogh, hoping to join him on the river. But instead Nuala comes in, and she and Brigit go through my book on Schiele and my newest one on Balthus.

"Some art," Brigit says with what sounds like informed authority full of scorn for amateurism. "These two sods are just obsessed with young girls playing with themselves. You couldn't hang these on the wall."

Museums, I mouth.

"None I've seen," Brigit says. "Anyway, I could see this sort of thing at home, if I was bent that way."

"What about the mirror by your bed? Means you're bent, does it?" Nuala says.

"Naw, that's just for the guys. They like to watch themselves, vain bastards."

Nuala's quiet. She's looking at *La Victime*, perhaps Balthus's most notorious work, next to *The Guitar Lesson*. Strong paintings, both of them. Naked adolescents. "Poor little girl," Nuala says. "A corpse already. I've seen better-looking corpses."

"I wish someone would explain art to me. I don't get it," Brigit says. "It seems to be whatever anybody says it is. This girl Nuala's looking at—it's just a dead teenager. She's right. We see them all the time. Drug overdoses mainly. Why is this art, and morgue photos are dirty secrets? Hell, why am I asking you? You couldn't answer even if you knew."

Damn Brigit! I wanted to shout at her. There were just a few principles to explain to her. I used to get the same shit down at the station from thick-necked cops, good guys but inclined to go physical in tense situations. They'd look at an abstract worth $150,000. "My kid could do that with his finger paints," they'd tell me.

There's something about some art that makes people hostile. They don't want to know what it is. They don't want to know what goes on in the minds of the people who create it, and the people who covet it.

But what I was discovering was more sinister, especially after yesterday on the river with Vincent. Except for a few cornfields, I saw that he seldom used yellow at all. That cheerfulness was my imagination. He layered on dull blues and greens, nothing very bright at all, even for faces. He depended on the haunting colors. I couldn't find the joy I remembered in his work. It made me wonder if any of the joy I remembered in my own life was true and bright, or if it had mainly been dark and dull.

The colors of Nuala's well.

"I've started taking classes, two nights a week at the New School," Nuala offers. "The first is art history; the second is color theory. I'm having more trouble with the theory class."

Then she says, for Brigit as much as me, "When I was a girl, my da used to say that the world was as wide for me as it was ever going to be. The older you become, he said, the more life narrows, until it's not much more than a box. And finally is nothing but a pine box under the sod."

Nuala got up to go.

" 'It's as wide as it's going to get, Nuala,' he'd say. 'Sail it wide, ride it broad, reach every corner that you're able. Then later, when the world's narrowing on you, your mind can sail and ride again.' "

She stood looking at Brigit and me from the doorway.

"I'm thinking maybe art is about pushing against the narrowing. The artists are trying to keep life wide for all of us."

20

MY BALLS TIGHTENED UP as close to me as they could. It was fear. I wasn't cold, though I was only wearing an overwashed cotton gown that tied together at neck and waist and left my ass bare. It was the same hospital gown that scandalized Cindy whenever it wafted open. It must have been designed for a purpose, though no one could say what it was.

I was on a fire escape in this gown, five stories above the street, trying to ease open the tight, creaky wood of Nuala's apartment window. The brittle flaking layers of old black paint on cold iron were scraping the soles of my feet. I was hoping that Sinead was a sound sleeper.

I reminded myself that it was 2:00 A.M. and I was lying flat in my bed attached to The Machine. This burglary of Nuala's place was only in my mind. Still, my balls stayed tight, and I could feel cold iron under my feet.

I wasn't in a coma. I was as lucid as I'd been in days. But I had resisted the sleeping shot because I was desperate to know how Nuala lived. I wanted so much to know her that way. You must see the things a person lives with to really know them; you must see how they live among their things, their relationship to their possessions. It gives you a real sense of someone's stance in the world. I knew a collector who refused to hang his best pieces in his Gracie Square apartment; he kept them under lock and key in storage. He seemed to do the same with most of his emotions, and with his sense of joy in life.

So I burgled Nuala's place.

It was astonishing. I came in through the living room window, and by the glow of the streetlamps I saw she had taken an ordinary, aging Village walk-up and made art of it, this girl who pretended to know so little, with her classes at the New School.

In New York you expect apartments to be awkward boxes, painted landlord-white down to the light switches and radiators. Nuala's main wall, with a brick fireplace in the center, was the rich charged yellow you find in lonely De Chirico cityscapes. She had massive wrought iron candlesticks with thick ecclesiastical candles four feet high. They would heighten that charge if you lit them and make the room begin to move. The wall facing the windows was a wonderful lime green I'd never seen anywhere, except maybe in St. Mark's Place boutiques. The window wall was electric blue, with the window frames done in the De Chirico yellow. The far wall, where the door to the bedroom was, was a mottled rusty ocher. It looked as if it had been sponged. And the ceiling was the palest, palest rose. I think she sponged it too.

She had no furniture in the usual sense. In front of the fireplace she'd put two ordinary lawn hammocks on lawn-green metal frames, next to a coffee table made of what seemed to be smashed automobile glass resting on Meccano set girders. A tiny brushed aluminum stereo was tucked in one corner. There was no TV. But there was a picnic table painted silver, surrounded by metal folding chairs—red, blue, yellow, black. A single calla lily occupied a Coke bottle in the center of the table. All the weight of this mad room was carried by a big, badly worn kilim with a lot of acid green and pink.

The CDs were in a stainless steel rack from the Museum of Modern Art: Nico, the Chieftains (no surprise), a disc by Hungarian Gypsies, *Turandot*, the Pretenders, Enya, the soundtrack to *Tous les Matins du Monde*, the Dave Matthews Band, Lyle Lovett, Gorecki's *Symphony No. 3*, the soundtrack to *La Double Vie de Véronique*, Nirvana *Unplugged*, Joan Osborne, something by Van den Budenmayer, some Beethoven piano sonatas. I imagined that her heart surged every time she listened to "Für Elise," like mine does.

On the kitchen counter there was only a gleaming chestnut box, which contained an almost complete set of old solid silver cutlery. No doubt a treasure from Ireland. The rest of the kitchen was pure Weber's: cheap blue Polish enamel pots and pans, a dozen plates, unmatched cups, a set of Mexican glass tumblers.

The wide-planked floor of the living room was cold. There was nothing on any of the walls except the ocher one. She'd hung a huge black-and-white poster of the top of the Chrysler building, unframed, with aluminum pushpins.

I had the urge to take off my gown before entering her bedroom, but it felt too creepy. So I slipped in quietly on my cold bare feet. The entire room, including the baseboards and ceiling, was painted a soft green-gray putty. Against one wall was a small chest of drawers, against another a yew bookcase—volumes of Pynchon, Joyce, Joseph Roth, Yeats, Jonathan Swift, Günter Grass, and every book John Grisham has ever written in paperback, as well as all four volumes of *Parade's End* and a pretty complete selection of le Carré. There were also John Berger's *To the Wedding* and Sebastien Japrisot's heartbreaking *A Very Long Engagement*. It was a library of sadness and pain, mostly, except for a tattered illustrated copy of *The Wind in the Willows*. They were books I knew well.

And in the very middle of the room, on another worn kilim, was an army cot. Its wooden legs and crosspieces were covered by precise folds of the most crisply ironed linen I'd ever seen. It looked like Nuala slipped in between the sheets so very carefully that she wouldn't make a wrinkle. And she hardly had. I could barely see her underneath all the linen and the billows of mosquito netting that hung around the cot from a hook in the ceiling. But her right leg from the knee down had worked its way from under the covers, which were pulled up to her nose. She slept as flat and motionless as I did back in the ICU. Sinead was snoring under the cot, no watchdog at all.

I had to speak to her. "Nuala," I whispered. "You must tell me things I need to know."

"Yes," she murmured, not moving. Her eyelids started rolling, as they do when we dream.

"Nuala, what's happened to me? What's left of me?"

"You'll make me cry. I don't want to cry anymore."

"Please."

"The last time you went out, the neurologist wrote you off. 'He'll never walk into my office,' he said. You weren't gone quite yet. But your body is shutting down bit by bit. Not enough oxygen."

"But I breathe. The Machine."

"The Machine helps you hold on. It can't save you."

"Am I dying?"

"Slowly. But so slowly nobody can be sure. The neurologist doesn't have any idea what's left of your brain. You could survive as a sort of vegetable, paralyzed from the waist down, maybe from the shoulders. You're breaking Brigit's heart too. You've fought so long."

"Nuala, what can I do?"

"Don't quit. Never quit. Keep your world as wide as you can. Wide and broad."

I kissed her forehead. There was no blue tube in my throat, no IVs in my arms. She tasted faintly of Nivea. She didn't even sigh. Sinead kept snoring. My scrotum was as tight as could be.

21

No one knows where we go when we dream. Science swears we are merely visiting that secret niche in our brain where we organize and file the impact of the day. Even though impossible things happen in dreams: You find yourself in other worlds; you talk to people you've seen buried. What's that got to do with filing, with organizing? There is no answer. But it is known that your body is paralyzed except for the almost ceaseless flickering of your eyeballs. Science tells us this.

So surely it was only a dream that I broke into Nuala's apartment and that Sinead didn't bark, and that Nuala spoke to me in her sleep. I don't believe in crap about your spirit leaving your body; I don't believe that my soul may have traveled to Nuala's. At most I believe your brain sometimes misfires. It's really only a chemo-electrical device after all. It can fool you about what's real and what's illusion.

But next day I couldn't help myself.

I stayed alert for any hint that what I had seen and heard was real. I wanted to know the color of her apartment walls, whether she really slept in a cot, and if she'd read the books I'd seen. I wanted to know if I'd seen Nuala in her private reality, where she was most her true self.

The place I saw last night was exactly the place I would like to live. People would say it was too young for me, more suited to an artsy girl.

I remember the top of her bookshelves. She'd arranged rows of bottle caps from odd brands of beer: Iron City, Anchor Steam, Genesee, Old Peculiar, Pete's Wicked. You could glue them all to a piece of painted masonite and frame it. People would call it art. I'd seen worse. A happening young dealer could have sold it. There was art in the kitchen too. An array of old-fashioned products that hadn't changed their labels in decades: Quaker Oats with the fat jolly Quaker, Cream of Wheat with the black man in white cook's clothes, Grandma Brown's baked beans, Arm & Hammer Baking Soda, Morton's Salt with the little girl under the umbrella.

Nuala was an artist and didn't know it (in my dream). Our little secret. Another world I'd made for Nuala. She and Vincent should have rowed away in that blue boat together. Neither of them was completely of this world. They saw another world the rest of us missed.

"NUALA'S GOT THE SNIFFLES," Brigit said when she came in that morning. "No good bringing her germs around. Sure we've plenty here, but she might have something fresh. You know what's back? TB! When I was young, I remember grand old Victorian places purpose-built as sanitariums for TB victims. They'd been empty for years. God knows, they might have to reopen them; the new stuff's drug resistant. We have to test everyone now.

"Didn't pee much last night, did you? You dehydrating on us?" Brigit asks, hefting my urine bag. It was a very dark yellow and less than half full. "And Christ on the cross, look at your feet. They're bloody filthy. Don't they bathe you anymore?"

I think Brigit may have already been to the nurses' bathroom that morning with one or two of her little needles.

"Have I told you I was an orphan? Grew up in a Dublin orphanage and they graduated me to nursing school when I was sixteen. We called the nuns 'penguins.' Don't all Catholic kids call them that? What I always wanted to know is why they were so cold and agitated if they were so happily married to Jesus. You think He put even a little smile on their faces? They looked like they lived with drunken longshoremen who beat them.

"Oh, there were a couple of exceptions, a little warmth and

compassion. That was mostly the young ones who hadn't had time to get bitter. But the ones I crashed into all seemed bitter about something. They tried to talk us into becoming nuns too, you know! Kept asking if you felt 'the calling.' I expect misery loves company. The only calling I felt was to get laid before I died dried up like one of them."

Success? I mouthed.

"No fear. Third night out of the orphanage, still in the nurses' school dorm then. It was in a dark doorway with a fellow I'd met in a pub, where else, standing up. It was a year or two before I got the real thing, realized how miserable that first time had been. Seemed OK at the time."

Brigit, you slut.

"Slut in training, buster," she said. "I haven't been around as much as all that. You're the real tomcat."

Me? I mouthed.

"Oh, yeah. We've been talking to our real cop friend at the Bells. He asked around—what else are cops good at? Christ, what a filthy reputation you've got: stupid six-foot models, grotty little art girls, old society ladies, a girl who used to cut your hair, shop girls of all kinds—met when you were buying presents for others, of course. You ought to be ashamed of yourself. Dozens and dozens, we're told."

Deeply ashamed, I am, I mouthed. And this God's punishment, yes?

"Don't ever say that!" Brigit said crossly. "I don't know where you stand on the afterlife, but just look the fuck around, buster.

This thing that's happening to you could just as easily have happened to a priest. Believe me, God hasn't put his finger on you just because you put your willie into a few more holes than you should've.

"It's a good thing you're an orphan too, come to think of it," she added. "Otherwise you'd be a real black sheep. The rest of the family would be wishing you dead for bringing the bad rain down on them."

Not exactly orphan, I mouthed. Brother and sister.

"So why doesn't anyone come to see you?"

Long story, I mouth.

"You've probably mortally insulted both of them at one point or another. You're a hard man."

Not lately.

Brigit started laughing. "I bet you dinner at French Roast that I could manage that."

Four Seasons, I mouthed.

"Now that would really be worth my while. I'll sneak up when the night shift is napping and we'll have a go."

Skip my shots tonight then.

"It won't matter, James. I can handle you just fine. Remember, I'm a trained nurse." She was giggling. I would have been giggling too, if I could have.

Brigit finished her chores—the ugly suctioning, adding the bitter orange to my milk shake, starting the first of the fentanyl. I waited for it to kick in like it seemed to have for Brigit, but it was pretty flat. Just a little warmth and then everything the same as before. Not more than a minute's euphoria. I envied Brigit, giggling madly as she left my room. I'd love to be high, do my mood good, I think. Here I was, every day getting thousands of dollars' worth of the newest, finest drugs available anywhere, and never a high. Just my luck. The best I could hope for was a foggy haze, kind of a six-tequila-shot stupor. Queasy. No fun at all.

BRIGIT AND NUALA had the next few days off. I had a nice visit from Myala; she had some good herbal therapies for Mr. Handsome Fellow. "You look a little like Imran Khan, our master cricket player, very handsome, only darker being Pakistani naturally. But colors are very nice," she went on, taking my hand. "Look at this nice difference, light and dark. Very artistic, aren't you agreeing?" I was thinking that if my body was in any shape at all, I'd bend this skinny thing right over the edge of the bed, lift her skirt, and show her some very artistic differences between light and dark. But there was nothing stirring as usual, despite her provocations and my unnecessarily prolonged glimpse down her blouse when she bent over to undo her therapeutic hookah. Her nipples were the exact shape, size, and color of deep red cherries. I'd never seen anything like them in my life.

Keep life wide, said Nuala's da, as long as you can before they box you up. I'm thinking that Nuala's da and Yeats had the right idea. And they certainly would have enjoyed a look at Myala's cherries.

But I missed Nuala and Brigit. They were the keepers of my

bearings. They set comfortable cycles for me. I could never seem to keep the rest of them straight; Susan sometimes on night shift and sometimes not, Patricia appearing here and there, a couple of middle-aged Filipinas who came late to give me morphine and anticlotting shots in the belly. They all took fine care of me, but they weren't friends in the way Brigit and Nuala were. It never occurred to me that it might be a one-way street.

HERE'S ALL I WANT: Nuala tells me all her secrets; I know her whole life. I try to tell her mine. I like her taste in shoes; I'm crazy about her apartment; I like everything about her, even her dark moods. We should be lovers by now. I'd pick her up after work. We'd see a movie, get some Thai takeout, and eat it on the garden swings in her living room. Or I'd lie in one of the hammocks while she slipped into a tight black dress and short boots and we'd go off to an art opening. The dealers always invited me: Free security, plus they might need my help one day. They knew no one would make me for a cop. I'd go off duty and unarmed, except for the usual snub-nosed .38 in an ankle holster.

And although I'd seen some wonderfully bitchy things go on at openings—an actual glass of champagne thrown in someone's face, and on one exciting occasion a six-foot-four black transvestite dressed in Versace ripping a Jil Sander top right off a model who couldn't have been more than seventeen (she had a pimple on one of her breasts)—none of it ever seemed anything but funny. Nuala and I would drink too much cheap champagne and enjoy ourselves immensely. Later, in our new double cot, we'd trash them all.

"And what's the use of perfect fake tits if you can still get pimples on them?" Nuala would ask. "Rather have me own pimples than silicone ones, any day."

Never once would we mention suctioning or the steel tubes in my chest or the way I couldn't control my bowels when I was unconscious. At most we'd laugh at something Miss Marriage or Brigit had done. We'd invite Brigit and her boyfriend of the moment over to my place for dinner every week or so. I was good in the kitchen and liked to show off from time to time.

This would be the time of falling in love, wouldn't it? The world would be so very wide that we'd know it went on and on and on, no horizons visible to our poor eyes. We'd have no notion of what was rushing in toward us, of what it could do. We'd have no fear.

22

THE NEXT MORNING that Brigit came in she was bubbling over with news. She couldn't seem to get the story out fast enough. It was finally over between Nuala and Ian. She'd kicked him out of her apartment at 2:00 in the morning, without his shoes! She threw the shoes down at him on the street. One hit him on the head. He begged her to let him back up so she could bandage the cut, but she refused. Brigit didn't want to go into the other details. She respected Nuala's privacy too much for that, she said. But apparently there was a fundamental sexual incompatibility. He kept asking something she wouldn't do. He also kept suggesting she paint her apartment off-white and get a futon to replace that cot. "The truth of it is, she hated his taste in shirts too much for it to go on." Brigit laughed.

Suddenly I'm on the blue boat with Vincent. Nuala *sleeps on a cot*! Her apartment *isn't off-white*! Something has happened. Vincent only nods. He keeps painting. He's doing stumpy peasants in a wheat field again. I'm inspired. I'm writing poems right there in the boat with Vincent. Yeats is pouring out of my pen. Time's no longer linear or mutable. Yeats never existed, you see, so it's up to me to fill the romantic hole his absence has left in the canon. It'd be ridiculed if I brought it back to 1995, of course; *The New Yorker* would never publish a line. But if I could leave it there with Vincent and get him to step ashore long enough to mail it to a Dublin publisher, it might do all right. If I brought just one back for Nuala, would she fall in love with me or sneer at it? You can't tell with modern girls. They might think it's too beautiful, not appropriate for the world that's ours now.

Nuala does have a *De Chirico yellow wall*! She has *lawn hammocks* in the living room and sleeps on a cot. She's read *Gravity's Rainbow*.

Brigit is my source. She wants to know how I live. That's the only opening I need. Small loft in Tribeca, I say, bought raw 1979. Dirt cheap. Not much—wall of books, leather sofa, two walls of windows, can see Hudson. Neighborhood spooky at first at night, but so what? Carry gun all time. Now full of Wall Streeters, lawyers, publishing people. Robert De Niro opened restaurant there. See movie stars on the streets.

What about her place? The usual, one-bedroom walk-up in the Village, landlord-white and furnished with whatever she could find on the streets.

Nuala? I mouth. Sounds strange.

"You wouldn't believe Nuala's place," Brigit says enthusiastically. "It's bloody fantastic; it could be in magazines. The walls are all different colors . . ."

Yellow? I mouth.

"Yeah, bright yellow, and one's lime, and she's got hammocks instead of sofas. The strangest thing is that she sleeps in a cot right in the middle of the bedroom, with the very fanciest sheets you ever saw. She's got lots of books, too."

Pynchon, Ford, Japrisot . . .

"Guys like that. She reads a lot. And she's got a great collection of beer-bottle caps from little local breweries. Not that she's so keen on beer. She just thinks the caps are beautiful."

All the loose plugs and sockets in my head are sparking like crazy. It can't be so. It can't be so. It can't be that I've seen all the things Brigit is describing. Can you really dream things you'll know in the future? I have to think that I am becoming demented.

Vincent, where are you and your little boat now? This is all much too strange for me anymore. I don't know what's happened. Maybe I've died. Maybe this is some weird afterlife, where things are familiar but not quite what they seem. I'm starting to sweat.

"You getting feverish again?" Brigit says. "Pulse one-oh-two, temperature one hundred even. Ah, you're getting overexcited.

Have another Ativan. I'll get Nuala to come and hold your hand for a while. That always calms you."

THERE IS A CHANGE. Something's gone wrong in the unmapped territory of my consciousness. The familiar world is skewed; my thoughts are tumbling over obstacles that have just appeared in a new channel. My ideas dip and break like rapids in a rising river. Or they freeze theatrically, like the Sunday mimes on the steps of the Metropolitan Museum of Art. I've blacked out a couple of times lately. Just for a minute or two, as if I'd been punched really hard. Shake it off like a boxer. It's nothing compared to those 104s with the eyes rolling back. These blackouts are too brief for any of the strange things I've lived in real comas. They're just lost moments, blanks. No trace once they're over, except that I feel wobbly in my head.

But it's a new thing for me. And any new thing is distressing.

Nobody's noticing but Nuala, and I'm not saying anything. Clare, who's surprised me by continuing to come by every now and then, accidentally gets a clue. She comes one evening (she's wearing a surgical mask in my room now, though all the nurses tell her it's not necessary). We're talking with the alphabet board and I've asked her to phone my brother and let him know my situation. Clare doesn't want to. She doesn't even know him, she says, and what's she supposed to tell him? Your brother's been in the ICU for a couple of months and finally thought you might want to know? No, it isn't AIDS—it's just chicken pox and complications—but he's still in critical condition, so if you want to see him you better come soon?

"How can I say that to your brother?" Clare asks. "You've been here sixty-nine days and just now you decided he should know? He'll hate me, he'll think it was me who hid it from him."

I won't see Clare after this, I'm pretty sure, if she does what I'm asking. I try to express this, I remember pointing at the I, and then everything goes black. I feel nothing anywhere; I hear nothing, not even my own heartbeat. I am aware that time is passing, but I feel outside of it, unconnected. It's not uncomfortable at all. But I reckon I ought to move my finger soon, before Clare gets confused. But I don't seem able to do this. Then Clare is shaking my shoulders. "Do you need the doctor? Shall I get the doctor?" she's saying. Her voice sounds panicky. "Do you feel all right? Is something happening in your head? I'm ringing for the nurse."

I shake my head no. I ask what happened.

"You pointed to the I and completely froze. Your eyes stayed open looking at the I, but they didn't move at all. I tried to talk to you but you didn't show any sign of hearing. Your hand was like ice. You just lay there pointing at that I, staring at that I," Clare says. "You never blinked, not even once.

"Oh, God," she says, starting to cry, "oh, Jimmy, I thought I was seeing death. Your damn death. God, why are we born if this is the way people we love end up?"

OK NOW. NOT DYING. STAY STRONG, I point.

"I'll call your brother tonight," Clare says. "I'll tell him to get his ass up here."

Susan comes in, and Clare tells her what just happened. Then she pulls her mask aside, kisses my lips, and leaves.

I DON'T BELIEVE there is one Death who comes specifically for you. Death is too busy everywhere at once. And sometimes it seems he has orders to be inventive, keeping whoever runs things amused. Or orders to provide those of us who will be surviving awhile longer with some lesson.

I hear about Death's odd antics every single lucid day. We have all-news radio. There are constant dispatches from the turbulent world outside: the clashes of nationalities in Bosnia, the movements of armies in Russia, the drug wars in Colombia, the petty congressional in-fighting in Washington. And always at least one instance of "the bus crash syndrome": Seventy-nine people killed today when Mexican bus plunges off mountainside.

Jokes or tragedies? There are reports too absurd to be real. Somewhere in India a troop of monkeys scamper over the tin roof of a country school, their combined weight causing the roof to collapse. Twenty-two children dead. A convict in Denver electrocutes himself trying to repair his radio while seated on the metal toilet seat in his cell. An eight-year-old girl climbing a large tombstone in an Iowa cemetery causes it to fall, crushing her best friend to death. In Zurich a father building a snowman accidentally buries his two-year-old daughter inside; she freezes to death. A Baltimore boy, whose mother had died eight months before, watches a bolt of lightning kill his father while they are visiting her grave. And another boy is walking home along a country road in Pakistan when a hawk, flying overhead with a krait in its talons, drops the deadly snake on him. It bites him and he dies on the spot.

You want to laugh . . . until you remember these were real lives. What if you knew them? Would it be ironic to anyone if I were to die of chicken pox, a kid's disease?

Not from Nuala's point of view. "Stop being so morbid, won't you?" she says. "You've a sick sense of humor, Mr. Blatchley."

Not humor, I mouth. Just never understood anything so real as these things.

"Name someone who has. Name someone who might explain any meaning to it all," Nuala says. "And you can't say 'God.' "

Van Gogh and Tolstoy, I mouth. Svevo, Shakespeare.

"Shakespeare, maybe," says Nuala. "The others, no. And even Shakespeare never understood the final thing about life."

Final thing? I mouthed.

"The end of it," Nuala says.

IT WAS NUALA who ratted me out to the neurologist about my blackouts. I'd taken to thinking of them as intermezzos. He had a fine time: some small tests he could do in my room, followed by the MRI, the hospital's equivalent of the space shuttle, with the doctor as astronaut. All they found was the same old neurological damage. Nothing new, no tumor, no aneurysm. Maybe it was time to change the drug mix. Maybe my body was too used to the current combination. Or allowing one drug to dominate, the unfortunate side effect being short-circuiting in my head, which led to blackouts.

So began the days of drug experiments. I was a veteran of most of them individually, but the new cocktails were fresh to my brain. A drug specialist assisted by Brigit and Nuala and the rest of the nurses began testing them out systematically. They were less interested in my subjective reactions—Dilaudid? Please, sir, may I have some more. Morphine? Very warm, very sleepy. Percocet? Baby aspirin—than the response of my blood pressure and heart rate and kidneys and my general alertness. They finally settled on a combination of fentanyl in the day and morphine at night for the painkilling, and a mix of an anticonvulsant called Klonopin and an antianxiety drug. This was to keep me calm enough so that I wouldn't pull out tubes and try to climb out of bed.

It was fine for a while.

IN THE GATHERING DIMNESS of dusk, Nuala comes and sits by my side. She takes my big, hot hand in her small, cool one and holds it as if it were a bird unable to fly. We don't talk. From time to time I look at her, I see her green eyes on my face. I look away. "This is the last thing I wanted," she says. "It can't come to any good. But you're learning me somehow. I don't know how you're getting to me. You're just another patient on The Machine. But if you had a heart, you'd break the connection before it gets any stronger."

My heart, such as it was, had gone missing a long time ago. It's only Nuala who's now bringing it back to me. How can I tell her that?

23

THE FOLLOWING SUNDAY began with a flurry of pampering. Brigit gave me a shave with a blue plastic disposable razor. She didn't bother to wear rubber gloves, but she still put the razor in the bin for hazardous waste. She did well. Not a knick worth noticing. Then she and Nuala unplugged all my IVs, stripped me, and gave me a fresh gown and a nice cotton bathrobe. They put plastic booties on my feet and reconnected the IVs at my wrists. Nuala gave my hair a stiff brushing. She washed my face and hands with a warm, sweet-smelling cloth. Then they lifted me off the bed and into my chair, arranging my blue tube to The Machine and my IV stands behind me.

It was a great confusion to me. It was a sprucing

up far beyond the usual. I suspected an inspection tour by some hospital executive.

"Your brother's coming up from Baltimore to visit you," Brigit said once I was settled. "Isn't that great?" It took me completely by surprise. I hadn't really believed Clare would phone.

"We thought you'd want to look your best." Nuala smiled.

I felt fresh and alert, though that faded as I waited. I managed to fill half my urine bag, which Nuala had hooked to the back of my chair so my brother and his wife wouldn't have to see it. Soon my ass was killing me, I wanted to get back in bed.

Then Richard walked in, looking like a healthy version of me, only three or four years older. But he was shockingly pale. He was wearing loafers, khakis, and a blue crew-neck sweater. He came right up and extended his right hand for a shake, which I could barely return. Joan was close behind him. She just squeezed my hand. I saw her looking at my weird brace, so I wiggled my left fingers.

"Hey, chief, how are you doing? You're looking good," my brother said. He didn't immediately realize I couldn't speak, and he handed me a vanilla milk shake that they'd brought as a treat. But Nuala told them what was what, and took the milk shake away before it made my hand too cold.

"So somebody finally shut you up. Ah, you never had much worthwhile to say anyway," Richard said, laughing. He took the milk shake from Nuala and began to drink it himself. He was a law-yer, with a reputation for aggressiveness. "When people hear I'm representing their opponent," he'd told me once, "they turn white." It was only half in jest. So I was pretty sure he had had a good talk with the doctor on duty before he'd come into my room. He wasn't the sort to turn white in the face himself, but here he was, pale even as he teased me.

"We thought we'd take you out to lunch but I'm told they don't trust you in a wheelchair. Too reckless," he said.

I grinned my lopsided grin.

Pencil-necked geek, I mouthed.

My brother looked completely blank. But his wife got it and giggled when she told him. She was better than he was at disguising her shock, and better at reading my lips too, so she was the translator.

But suddenly there was nothing for her to interpret. My eyes began to well over with tears and my lips trembled. I was furious with myself. I blamed Nuala for not giving me a shot of something before they'd arrived. It was shattering to see them there looking so normal, so much the same as they'd always looked. My brother was wearing the exact type of khakis and sweater he'd been wearing for the past twenty-five years. He still had what I'd always called his TV weatherman's haircut, with some hair just covering the tops of his ears and falling over his forehead. For years I'd been telling him to do something about that hair. Aside from the hair and my haggardness, we looked so much alike. Brigit was outside the room checking him out through the window. Nuala stood behind me, in case I needed any help.

So glad to see you. Been lonely, I mouthed. Richard's wife took my right hand and held it from then on while she repeated everything I tried to say.

Like getting hit by a truck, I mouthed. Never imagine such a thing can happen.

"If it was an accident at least I could sue the hell out of the driver," my brother said, grinning but still paler than ever. I sensed an undercurrent of real rage that he had no one to strike out at. "A couple of million, easy."

When I was young, before our lives diverged, my brother had always been a big brother, in the best sense. It was his role, as he saw it, especially after our father died. Nobody would mess with me in high school because they knew they'd have to deal with him. And when he went off to college he used to invite me down for football weekends, to teach me the proper way to get drunk at fraternity parties, for when my time came. But mainly he tried to give me the advantage of his only slightly greater experience when I was going through the rough spots.

I'd always felt that feeling remained, even as our actual contact diminished over the years to a phone call every couple of months. I felt I could depend on him if I needed him.

"Happened to run into the doctor outside and had a chat," Richard said. "He says your lungs are healing nicely, and you're breathing a bit on your own. They may be able to disconnect the ventilator in a couple of weeks. Sounds good, doesn't it, chief?"

I nodded.

"And they don't foresee much permanent nerve damage, or any

permanent damage at all actually except some scar tissue on your lungs, which won't amount to anything. With a little luck, we'll be sailing together by the end of the summer," he lied.

My eyes betrayed me again, and I started to choke. "Please look away a minute," Nuala said, quickly unhooking my blue tube and inserting the suction. Richard obeyed, but I saw his wife's eyes widen at the slop Nuala sucked out.

Nothing, just phlegm, I mouthed, and Joan repeated this, trying to sound casual.

"Hey, we brought you something you'll get a kick out of," Richard said, reaching into a Barneys bag and pulling out a large album. "Just a little thing we put together over the past few evenings. Thought it might make you smile."

Nuala and Joan propped the heavy album up on my lap, and I was able to turn the pages with my right hand. They'd scavenged all their old boxes of photos and made a sort of story of my life, our broken family's life. I wanted to make a joke about your life flashing before your eyes, but I decided Joan might not be up to translating that. And maybe it wouldn't be funny to them. I could feel their eyes as I leafed through. I could feel their hope that I'd enjoy the little world they'd made for me. I smiled as broadly as I could.

They'd made something to smile over. On the first page there was a tiny black-and-white photo of me at about six, wearing a complete baseball uniform and awkwardly swinging a bat. There was one of my grandfather holding my hand as we jumped off a jetty into the Chesapeake Bay. I couldn't have been more than seven, with long skinny arms and legs all splayed. There was a snap of me and my brother in our midget football uniforms. I was about ten, and he was twice my size. My little sister was in the middle looking adorable, holding the ball. I was wearing a black jersey—number twenty-one, Loch Raven Kiwanis Club. There was a shot of my father and my grandfather from the '40s when my parents had only recently gotten married, grinning like best drinking buddies on the back porch of my granddad's house. There was a shot my evil brother had taken when I broke my nose at twelve playing soccer, and the whole thing was pushed over in front of my left eye. I looked like an underage boxer. There was a shot of me in a Speedo at my first swimming pool lifeguard job one summer. I had great muscles then; I looked immortal. "Wait a second," Nuala said when I tried to turn that page. "Look at those arms!"

Richard and Joan laughed. "He was a wrestler in high school, always pumping iron," Richard said. "Lacrosse and football too. But kind of wimpy, anyway. Neck like a stack of dimes."

There was a photo of me at seventeen standing proudly beside my first car, a used '64 maroon Corvair convertible with a black top. And a truly laughable one: me in a rented tux, long-necked and awkward, standing next to my prom date. I think her name was Georgette. She had beautiful breasts that her dress only hinted at (but which I later got to feel up). Her hair was piled up in the highest beehive you can imagine. The classic senior prom photo.

On the last page was an eight-by-ten that stirred so many memories it felt like I might have a seizure. I had no idea that Richard and Joan had a copy. I was twenty-two, wearing cowboy boots and tight jeans, a cigarette dangling from my lips. I was squinting a little into the light, my hair thick and wavy and more than halfway down my back. I had two black Nikons slung around my neck. I had just gotten out of college and was working as a newspaper photographer for $110 a week. Next to me was the girl whom I thought was the love of my life. A tall thin girl with a spray of freckles over her nose, the blackest hair, the bluest eyes and a body as graceful as any dancer's. She leaned into me, her arm around my waist. "Hold on," Nuala said when I tried to turn that page. "She must be Scottish, with that hair and skin. You're well rid of her."

Richard and Joan laughed now.

They left shortly after that, because they had a long drive back to Baltimore. Richard tried to shake my hand again in his hearty, professional style, and shook Nuala's too. Joan kissed me on the cheek. She said, "Don't worry. The worst is already passed."

AND I WAS ALONE AGAIN.

My ass was on fire from sitting so long, and my neck was wobbly. I begged Nuala and Brigit to put me back in bed. And then I just lay there. I couldn't stop weeping. It wasn't that I was afraid to die or that I thought I'd never see them again. I wept because I'd been reminded that I was connected to the world by blood. There was a place for me in it, and people who would miss me if I were to go. And I had wasted so much time with people and things that counted for nothing.

I was also crying for the beautiful black-haired girl. We lived together for two years right after college. I'd thought we had plans for a lifetime. If you're determined, you can conclude your present situation is inevitable by tracing all the events of your life, all the years and years of actions and choices, that led up to today. If I did that, I would conclude that it was Jennifer the black-haired girl who started me on my way to the ICU. But it's a ridiculous exercise.

Instead, I think about our life together. I remember nights in front of the fire, holding each other, listening to some obscure English rock band: "You come right inside of me/Close as you can be/You kiss my blood/And my blood kiss me."

I felt that close to her. I thought we were as close as two people could ever be.

I'll never know how much she lied. It's not important now. But for years I was obsessed with knowing when exactly she knew we had no future, when exactly she started sleeping with other men, whether she still loved me when she encouraged me to go back to school for an M.A. and then a Ph.D. in art history, when exactly she decided that at the end of my first year she would leave me, with half an M.A. and no choice but to go work for a living again.

But that was only the surface of things. What really troubled my mind were the unanswerable questions: Had it been a real connection or not, was it one-way or two-way, and what went wrong?

I was so young, immature. She knew so much more than I did. She could have been softer with me. Instead, I felt like she waited until I was most vulnerable. Years later I thought I'd become as good a judge as any man of the depth and intensity of a woman's feelings. And I ignored those feelings when I wanted out or wanted to take advantage of a situation. I was stupid enough, for a while, to believe I had earned the right to be cruel.

But things were different now.

I'd concluded that Nuala and I were made for each other, even if she didn't see it yet. I'd have to work hard. But I was sure I could do it, once I had my health back. It wouldn't be a matter of seducing her; that wasn't the key to Nuala. It would be making her really believe what I really believed: That we'd been waiting all our lives to come to each other.

I WANTED TO WRITE A NOTE to Richard and Joan, but I couldn't control my right hand well enough to even sign my name. I thought about asking Brigit or Nuala to help.

They stopped by on their way home, already dressed for the street. "Good day today, buster? Boy, if your brother was ten years younger, watch out, he'd be in trouble around here."

"Brigit, you're impossible." Nuala laughed.

"You look sad," Brigit said. "Time for your fentanyl?"

Photos sad, I mouthed.

"They were lovely," Nuala said. "You looked great. Such a cute kid, even cute as a hippie. I bet the girls were all over you."

Another life, I mouthed. All gone.

"At least you've got something to remind you. All I've got is two snaps. My family didn't have a camera. And I didn't have a hippie brother photographer messing around with Scottish models, who, by the way, are well known to be loose," Nuala said.

You still in diapers when I was in love with that girl. Wanted to marry her, I mouthed. She left me.

"Pretty insensitive, Nuala! Getting in a little dig over the heartbreak," Brigit said.

Nuala looked at her feet, like a shy girl who's embarrassed by some attention she's getting.

Like to see your pictures, I mouthed.

"One of these days, maybe," Nuala said. "But you should ask Brigit. She always lets her boyfriends photograph her in her birthday suit."

"Only on my birthdays," Brigit said. "And those are private."

ONE OF NUALA'S DAYS turned out to be about a week later. While Brigit was busy at the other end of the ward, Nuala brought me a little brown kraft-paper envelope and shyly handed it to me. Then she stood by my bed. "They're no good," she said. "But that's all there is."

I took the two black-and-whites out of the envelope. They had deckled edges, the way photos here were made in the 1950s. In the first, a Nuala of about nine or ten was standing on a wooden dock in a child's one-piece bathing suit. She was skinny as a stick, but hip-shot exactly the way young women stand when they're leaning against a railing trying to look attractive. Her hair was wild in the wind, her thick eyebrows were absolutely straight lines above her huge eyes. And she was looking directly at the camera with an expression that could have been disdain or pure instinctive seductiveness, a precocious awareness that men would want her. The second was more ordinary but had the same power: Nuala on the steps of her school at about fifteen, wearing a navy jumper with a white blouse under it. Her face was partially shaded by a straw hat that was obviously part of her school uniform. The skirt was long, but you could see the curve of muscle in her calves, and on her heavily eyebrowed face, in those still-enormous eyes, was the same womanly expression, that same intense sexuality that she keeps so well hidden now.

I'd have proposed, I mouthed.

"And my da would have laughed that a scamp like you would even dare, and the rest of the village would have thought you mad, and scandalous for wanting a mere girl."

Beautiful girl. But you had the eyes of a woman, I mouthed.

"Maybe I knew things. Maybe I was a wise child."

You seemed to know what you'd want, what you'd become.

"So how did I lose that? Why do I feel like a green girl all over again?"

I didn't know her losses. I couldn't say a thing.

24

THE HOWLING BEGINS when the sun goes down. It doesn't matter if there's a moon or not. Night after night this soul-killing, agonized screaming comes from a young man farther down the ward. He isn't on The Machine. But he's HIV, which is why he's in the infectious ICU. I've never heard a sound before that literally chilled my bones, but the wails and moans and shrieks of this man does it. No matter how many blankets are put on my bed, I remain shivering, sleepless, anticipating each howl in the moments between them. This, I thought, is what hell sounds like.

He's suffering from AIDS dementia. Surely there is something in the hospital's vast repertoire of narcotics that can ease him. There is not, Brigit tells me, because the howls and shrieks have no cause. In fact, since he doesn't even know he's making them, sedation would be useless. Only full anesthesia might quiet him, but you can't keep anyone under anesthesia night after night.

By the sixth night of this, I feel like I'm losing my own mind. Around 3:00 in the morning, the wretched shrieks echoing through the ICU, I ring for a nurse. Susan comes. I ask for my alphabet board.

CAN'T YOU HELP HIM? CAN'T YOU MAKE HOWLING STOP? I BEG YOU.

Susan looks at me quizzically, checks all my meters and lights, quickly takes my temperature. Everything's all right. The drips are dripping at the right rate, and The Machine is damply huffing.

Susan looks into my eyes. "He died two days ago. His bed is empty. Do you understand? He's dead."

THE NEUROLOGIST WAKES ME up the next morning. Here's a fine reason for more tests: A fellow keeps hearing a sound two days after it's stopped. A challenging case. That's why the doctors come so quickly to see me and are so frank. But he can find no reason why I should've heard the howling. And he cannot tell how scared I am now of my own mind.

The next night, on all the same drugs, I hear nothing but the muted noises of the ward: the occasional groan, the breathing of The Machine, the sound of a suctioning, the rubbery footsteps of the nurses, the sound of pills jiggling in paper cups on steel trays (for those who can swallow), and the cold clicking of needles (for those who can't). I'm getting shots between my fingers these days, just like Brigit. But you can see why: my arms are a mass of tiny white scars, not a visible vein anywhere. They've almost ruined my beautiful Chinese tattoo. Only Nuala ever bothers to avoid the delicate characters.

Nuala and Brigit know all about my episode. I fear I'm becoming psychotic. "No such luck for you, buster. You're as sane as we are. You were just hearing an echo, like an image from a nightmare that slips back into your head a couple nights later. Nothing to worry about."

"It happens to sensitive types," Nuala says.

"And you're the type who gets misty over Van Morrison tunes, aren't you? You imagine Dolores O'Riordan or Sinead O'Conner is singing to you. We know your type, all right."

"There was one guy here last year who kept begging Brigit to sing Gaelic love songs to him," Nuala says.

"Like I was Enya or something. Like a Dublin girl ever learns a line of Irish. Hicks like Nuala might know some Irish, but not us city girls."

"Only my grandda spoke it to my grandma, when he wanted some privacy. The rest of us could hardly understand," Nuala says.

I gesture for my alphabet board. Then I write TA MO CHLEAMHNAS DEANTA.

"That's impossible," Brigit says. "You can't know Irish. I'd bet next week's pay on that. What's it mean, Nuala?"

" 'My match it is made,' " Nuala says, looking at me in an odd way, then blushing.

"So let's have some more. Let's see how sensitive you can be," Brigit says.

IT HAD BECOME A GLIMMERING GIRL.

"No, in Irish, Yeats doesn't count. Something in the 'ta mo' line. Woo us a bit," Brigit says.

IRISH JUST CHIEFTAINS' SONG TITLE. DON'T KNOW ANY MORE.

"Ah, ya rat-faced deceiver," Brigit says, laughing. But Nuala doesn't look very pleased. I don't get a smile from her when they leave my room.

But on her final check that evening, Nuala bends close and whispers in my ear: " 'Si an bhean a dhfhag mo chroi craite.' And that's a friendly warning you might heed before you go fooling with an Irish girl again."

I tried it on a couple of Irish nurses on the night shifts, but I couldn't spell the words exactly right, or mouth them clearly enough to be understood. The one who did speak Irish most fluently said it sounded something like "Your ear will go to France alone."

But I was determined to learn what Nuala had said—and to answer her.

Finally I thought of looking at the Chieftains' CD, where I'd gotten the song title. The lyrics were printed in English and Irish on the inside jacket. The minx had quoted back to me the very last line of my song.

When Nuala came into my room the next time, I gestured her to come close. And then I mouthed: She's the wee lass that's left my heart broken. She smiled brightly. Then, with the alphabet board, I spelled out CHUALA ME AN SMOILIN'S AN LONDUBH A RA/GUR EALIAGH MO GHRA THAR SAILE—"I heard the blackbird and the linnet say/ that my love had crossed the ocean."

Nuala's smile vanished. "But mine's right here," she lied. "Not in this room, of course. Mine lives across the river in Brooklyn. Here there's only an ill fella too clever for his own good."

How ill, Nuala? I mouthed. Checking out?

"Don't ever put your mind on that. Be thinking of living. When you get out I'll introduce you to a nice Irish girl. Or Brigit will. Or maybe you'd like Brigit herself, lovely thing."

Drugs, I mouth.

"Brigit'll be all right. It's not unusual for people who work in hospitals. Just keep it to yourself, and we won't tell anyone what you get up to with your hands when you're really drugged."

Such as?

"Well, the only thing that wouldn't get you arrested is the way you try to grab our hands when we leave. Like a bloody Frenchman, you are, for hand-kissing. The rest? Too filthy to mention. Cindy is thinking of suing you. Don't worry, it'll all come out in court. You're a cop, you must know a good lawyer."

Nuala could barely contain herself now, her good spirits. I must have seemed comical at times. Really fucking comical.

I STARTED DRIFTING, the way I often do in the afternoons. I close my eyes and see things. Sometimes a world I've made for Nuala, or for a long-lost love, or even one I've really lived in. Today it's one of mine.

I was nineteen when cancer began to gnaw my grandfather's stomach. I went to his room right after his surgery, as soon as they'd moved him out of recovery. As he came to his senses, he recognized me. He went straight for the drainage tube sutured into the slice they'd made in his belly, tugging at it. He tried to rip out his IVs. "Help get me out of here, Jimmy," he said in a plaintive voice. "You've got to help me out of here." I called a nurse to calm him down. She sedated him mildly enough so that he gave up his escape but could still talk a bit. And when I went to see him the next day, he seemed exactly his old self. A few days later I took him home, and he talked about all the improvements he was going to make to his house.

Then I went back to school for a few months. When I came home for spring break, I didn't go to my mother's house but directly to my grandparents'. I saw a smallish man trying to drive nails into a new plank on the back porch. The cords in his thin neck stood out with the effort of each blow. It was an ordinary hammer, ordinary ten-penny nails, but the hammer seemed so heavy for him. He bent nail after nail, not striking a single solid blow. He finally threw down the hammer in disgust. "Dad-dad?" I said. He looked at me for the first time. He'd lost thirty or forty pounds. The man who all my life had been big and active now looked cadaverous and fragile.

"Jimmy," he said. "Damn hammer's no good anymore."

We went inside and my grandmother gave me a beer with sardines on saltine crackers, the usual lunch for my granddad and me. But Granddad could only have tea and toast. I could see his blue veins throbbing through the thin skin of his temples. "Damn hammer," he kept muttering. After lunch, he napped on the sofa. I went out and finished planking the porch. When he saw it, he said, "So you went and got a better hammer?"

"No, Dad-dad," I said. "I just saw the way it was bent and hit the nails at an angle to compensate. They're all in now."

"Christ, Jimmy, don't ever get like me. Let yourself die before you let them cut out your stomach."

He was seventy-two.

About a month later, they took my granddad to the hospital in the middle of the night and he died. That day on the porch was the last I'd see him, a wasted man trying to hammer in some nails.

Then I was crying, for him and myself and people everywhere whose bodies were letting them down. I hadn't cried in more than twenty years, not since before my father's funeral when I was fourteen, until I got into this hospital. It had nothing to do with pain; I could take any amount of pain. But I figured the drugs were doing something to loosen my emotional control. I'd had a lot of control, once. Too much, some women said.

I was just wiping away the tears when Susan walked in at the start of her shift. Brigit went over my dials and IVs and charts with her. It was handover time. With Susan that was OK, because she was pretty and smart and I liked her. With some of the others, it felt like abandonment. How easily I rested depended on who had duty that night. Susan had seen me wipe the tears. She'd find time to come by for a chat later on.

I hated the dusk, an hour I once loved.

I felt so lonely now when the world spun into darkness. There was no one person in my life who was close enough to connect me to it. That's all it takes: one person with whom you've no barriers at all. That joins you to the world and makes everything else possible. Brothers don't count. It's terrible not to have that person. You spend all your life searching. I'd found Clare, and I thought she would save me. She did for a long while. I don't think most people get lucky. I think they live just as alone as they die.

It's hard to talk about such ideas, with the limits of the alphabet board. No tones, no emphasis, no subtleties at all. Just simple statements. But Susan tries hard and usually gets the drift. I'm telling her about my grandfather and the one real person you need in your life, and I think she's understanding me.

"Maybe the one you need always finds you," she said. "Maybe it's futile to search at all, because you're going to be found."

Nice idea. But when?

"When it's your time. Not before or after. When it's your time," Susan said.

They said that a lot around the hospital. They said it whenever someone died, and whenever they had no real answer to give.

25

"TIME, GENTLEMEN."

Probably the most used words in England, after "I," "me," and "bloody fuckin' hell." I don't like any of them much.

"Time, gentlemen." Treacly; it makes me want to wash my hands. The words're even part of the poetic canon, put there by a bankteller who became a famous poet once a greater poet took him in hand, a man who had his wife committed to an insane asylum so he could lead the "artistic" life he required. I prefer the bluntness of "bloody fuckin' hell."

I am interested in what time it is for me, naturally. Is the clock still running strongly, or is it almost wound down? Is the second hand about to make its final, startling stop, the one that makes us shake the watch and look again for movement? It's getting harder to care. But I do guess it's past time to forget things like putting Nuala in a whitewashed cottage with starched lace curtains. Time to forget picture postcard Ireland.

For Nuala and Brigit, it's time to take the shiny steel elevator down ten floors, navigate some illogical corridors, and walk out into the spring sun of New York. Maybe they'll just go up the block to the coffee shop for grilled cheese sandwiches and tomato soup. Or they'll walk down to Sixth Avenue and have a chicken and avocado salad at French Roast. Who can say? What does it matter? It's only lunch and there's always tomorrow. And the milk shakes keep flowing down the tube in my nose. The Machine keeps pumping. Maybe time has finally stopped. Ah, but that would be too much in my favor.

How does Nuala measure her time? In patients come and gone, weekly shifts over and done, books read, films seen, men met, love made? Brigit is just racing; her life's a blur of risks taken and survived. She has no more idea what time it is than I do, and she cares less.

Nuala wants friends, I think. She wants to see some new art, see some new theater, listen to some new music, really live in this big city where there is that critical mass of all sorts of people that produces real creation.

But mostly she wants friends at home in this metropolis, good friends she can entrust with her secrets and share what's new that comes along. And maybe later, a husband and a baby, and a life in which people maintain their curiosity and have conversations and don't settle for television or the consolations of a Guinness or an Irish bar where some are drunk on nostalgia from the moment they enter.

The worlds I've made for Nuala are not the ones she wants. They're my own fantasies, the ones that come from my own weariness after so many years in the big city. I was weary long before I came to the ICU. She doesn't care about the damp Irish cottage, the farmhouse in Tuscany I dream of, or the one in upstate New York that I actually own. She doesn't want a flat in London or Paris. And she doesn't want me. I'm a professional responsibility, and she's faithful to her duty. Brigit might flee with me; the racey ones are often those who most want a quiet life but have no idea how to find it. Brigit has never gotten over her forced, relentless path through the orphanage, nursing school, the ICU.

But Nuala wants life, lots of it.

Nuala fights thinking of death. She sees it too often. I think she tries to believe it's just a deeper sleep, except that you never see the sleeper again. It probably took her years on the job to develop this skill. No one naturally shrugs off witnessed death. But this kind of evasion can't work in your life. I think with Robbie her whole world crashed into a black void from which she believes it might never emerge.

Back into the black well. Poor Nuala.

It's quiet Nuala who needs a wider world, the varied minds, the ideas that collide and reform and express themselves in another form. It's Nuala. She loves a good lively dinner party with people she's just recently met. She loves to pull on her boots and take

Sinead for a walk and meet a Rasta poet in Washington Square Park selling mimeographed volumes of his work. It excites her, the way creativity always does those who haven't yet found the key to their own.

Like me. I used to haunt the Strand bookstore on Broadway, buying cheap used art books. I filled a wall of shelves with them. And in better days, when I wasn't out with Clare trying to get laid, I'd spend hours on my sofa looking at what artists can do. I particularly liked the volumes on a single artist, so I could trace the development of ideas and skills. But I also liked the books on collections that showed me the vastness of possibility painting has. Only death stops most artists. There is no natural end of creativity.

Except that death is natural.

Death is "Time, gentlemen." We all hear it. I want it to roar, to demand.

I've heard it once, but only in cajoling whispers. It can't possibly be my time yet. I haven't created anything. I've never done anything worthwhile in my life. I've only just been collecting experiences. And sometimes I think I only did that so I'd have my wall-full of memories, like my wall of art books, so that I could lie in bed at night and call them up—study them, the line and passages of them, the colors and tones.

The dark little Slovene I slept with one night in the Julian Alps and never saw again.

The Park Avenue matron who'd arranged to have one of her Old Master drawings stolen. She told me my Italian suit was rather too flashy, didn't I think, when I pointed out the implausibility of her story and the penalties for insurance fraud.

The two Puerto Rican kids who tried to mug me on Lafayette Street; instead of simply arresting them, I beat them both bloody with my pistol butt and left them pissing in their pants on the sidewalk.

The flight into foggy Milan where we missed the runway on the first pass. And, as the 747 pulled back up, straining at full power, I prayed like a choirboy afraid to die.

The blind date on which I took home the blind date's best friend, and kept her there, happily nude for most of two days.

The particular smell of the cheeseburgers at Odeon at 2:00 in the morning.

The first cigarette after leaving the dentist high on nitrous oxide.

The first time I lectured a group of rookie cops and realized they were almost young enough to be my sons.

The first time I took a pretty girl to bed and couldn't get an erection.

I look at Nuala now on days when I'm lucid, and I feel glad that she has all the time in the world. At least I pray she does. Anything could happen, I've learned that. But I pray nothing stops her from wearing her motorcycle boots until there are holes in the thick soles, or from walking Sinead until the dog's too old to walk and has to be put down, or from raising a girl of her own who grows up scrappy and freckled and wild-haired and breaks a dozen hearts—here in America, not in the dank well of Irish failure. Maybe when she's lived in America long enough, she'll realize it can be a well too, but she'll know how to stay lucky, up in the light, in the free life.

All Nuala really has to learn is her effect on people. She believes she's just an ordinary girl, plainer than many, nothing special at all. A little too dark in her moods sometimes, or shy with her feelings. She underestimates herself. She thinks she's just another boring Catholic girl. She doesn't realize the pull of her spirit and her mind. And no one is going to convince her differently. I think she's carried Robbie around for so long because she felt grateful to him for loving her.

She didn't know at all how grateful he ought to have been.

THERE WAS ONLY EVER one real thing I was able to do for Nuala, and I couldn't even do it myself. There was an Italian punk living on her block, all balls. Every time he saw Nuala coming home, usually late at night, he'd taken to shouting out his window at her—what you'd guess, crude remarks about her body and what he'd like to do with it. More filthy than the usual stuff though. "Cold bitch," he'd call out. "Lesbian," when she ignored him. It shook her, this boy and his bad mouth. Brigit told me so. So with my board and Brigit, I wrote a note to Joey Cigna, my friend in Homicide. Joe was a guy who, twenty years on, still referred to "The Nam." He never spoke of what he'd seen or done there. I was pretty sure he had good reasons to keep quiet. He followed Nuala home one night and heard the guido giving her a hard, dirty time. He was sitting on his stoop, not leaning out his window. Joey muscled him up against a parked car as soon as Nuala disappeared into her building.

Brigit smuggled him in to see me the next day, claiming he was my first cousin.

"Jesus, Jimmy, you look like dogshit." He walked in, belly straining the button of his sports coat. "You look almost as bad as a guy I knew named MacAlary. A mine ripped off his balls and created him a new asshole. But that was exceptional. Hey, you need anything? They taking care of you OK? Anything I can do for you?"

I smiled, but I could feel water rising in the corners of my eyes. With Brigit and my board I told him I'd be up in a few weeks and could still take him down anytime I wanted. He laughed. And then I thanked him.

"It wasn't nothing. He was just a dumb kid, feeling tough. I ID'd myself as a cop and had my Glock stuck in my waistband where he could see it—and feel it when I leaned on him. I says, 'It would be wise of you to keep your dirty gumbah mouth off the nurse.'

"He says, 'What nurse? I don't know no nurse.'

" 'That's right,' I says. 'You don't know no nurse, you never saw one on this block, and you're never gonna see one for the entire rest of your shitty life. In fact, you ain't gonna see any females at all around here. They're gonna be like ghosts, invisible, see?

" 'And guess what I'm gonna do if I hear you putting your dumb guinea mouth on her again? I'm gonna come down here angry. And I'm gonna cuff you and search you. And surprise, surprise! Guess what I'm gonna find in your pockets? A crack pipe, and enough vials of rock for you and all your gumbah friends.

" 'And you're goin' straight to Riker's on a felony for dealing, capice? Some big nigger out there's gonna make you his wife the first night.' "

Joey starts laughing. "The guy pissed himself right there. He turned crack white and pissed himself. He said 'I'm not seeing nobody or saying nothin'. No way, man. I swear on my mother's grave.' The dumb fuck's mother probably isn't even dead yet. He's seen too many movies."

He and Brigit have a laugh that must go on for five minutes.

Then Joe just looks at me for a while. I'm smiling big at him. But he's looking at the blue tube and the IVs and my wasted face, and he knows. He's seen plenty of stuff like this. He knows, but he'd die before he'd say one thing true about it. He grips my shoulder with his meaty hand so hard I wince. "Pussy," he says, grinning at me. "Just hang tough. Don't mean nothing, Jimmy. Don't mean nothing. Drive on. I'll see you down at the precinct pretty soon. You need anything, anything at all, Brigit knows where to get me now. I hope she don't forget I'm available too, there's anything she might want."

They grin at each other.

IT'S THE MIDDLE of the night. Patricia comes in to give me some morphine. I'm wishing instead for the pleasure domes of opium, the extravagant dreams of Kublai Khan. She checks my IVs, my blue tube. She gives me a little suctioning to ease the flow of air. The clock says 3:00 A.M. It mystifies me that I should be more clear-headed now than I am at most hours of the day. But this is the hour when the drugs are at their lowest ebb. Maybe they don't realize that nothing much sedates me, and the sleeping shots are not much more than aspirin to my skewed metabolism.

Never mind. I think at night. I doze away the days. I just like to be alert when Brigit and Nuala are around. I want them to see me as a man, with intelligence and humor, not just a semi-comatose lump, one step up from vegetative. I wonder what Nuala looks like in her short skirt and motorcycle boots. Did I see her one night like that? I can't remember. I wonder if men she and Brigit meet are ever afraid when they learn they're nurses, if they fear of some sort of contamination? Men are so full of irrational dread they never admit.

I sleep right through Brigit and Nuala's first check the next morning. The warm sun on my face can't disturb me. I'm off in a darker place—not frightening but not a blue May day in New York.

When I do awake, I see from my window a crew putting tar paper on a brownstone roof below. They're very efficient, swabbing down the glue and unfurling the thick, black rolls. They're finished by about 2:00, but one stays behind to coat the black tar with a silver reflective paint. Keeps the upper floor cooler, I suppose. I was only a little foggy, and I could see that he was working a pattern out from the center toward the edges. The silver was brilliant to see, covering up the black. I imagined the satisfaction of each stroke. But as he got nearer and nearer the roof's perimeter, something seemed out of place. And at the end, I saw that he had painted himself into a corner opposite from the corner with the fire escape he was supposed to climb down. He stood there for a minute, angrily banging his roller on the roof. And then, resigned, he simply walked backward, from his corner to the fire escape corner, dragging the roller behind to cover up his footsteps.

It's something funny I would have liked to tell Brigit and Nuala. They'd have laughed and said the painter was probably a dumb Mick. But it was too complicated for me to mouth, or relate on my alphabet board. When they came to my room on their way out that evening, though, I asked for the board.

TIME, GENTLEMEN.

They did laugh at that. "Not for us," Brigit said. "The Bells'll be open for hours yet, and I'll drink a Guinness for you."

Nuala surprised me. "I'll meet you in a bit, Brigit. I want to talk to James."

"OK," Brigit said, with a sly smile.

"I went to a movie last night," Nuala began when Brigit had disappeared. "I wish there was some way you could see it. It was called *Wings of Desire*. There were dozens of angels who lived in Berlin, watching everything. One of them wants very badly to experience human life, instead of the sort of cold, timeless immortality that angels have."

Good concept, I mouth. Movie any good?

"The strangest I've ever seen. The angels are invisible, naturally, to those round them. But we see them on screen like ordinary men and women, all wearing drab overcoats and doing nothing much—wearily wandering the city, observing what goes on, and then getting together to tell each other what they've seen."

Recording angels, I mouth.

"And nothing more. Nothing at all. They can't help anyone. They whisper into people's ears when they're about to die, and it makes no difference. They can't do anything. They can't stop tragedies or save anyone. They're like eternal witnesses to all the sadness of life.

"And they have no wings."

The one who wants to be human? I mouth.

"He's allowed to. He has to give up his immortality as the price. At first he's delighted—he's like a baby seeing everything for the first time. He has no idea what's bad or dangerous. And he falls in ecstatic love with a trapeze artist at a ratty little circus."

How German, I mouth. Nuala doesn't smile.

"I've never believed in angels or anything. I'm a poor Catholic for sure. But I'd always secretly hoped for a great benevolence somewhere," says Nuala, her eyes full.

"And it was only a movie. But what if it's true? It means there's no one to turn to, no one to look out for us. We're entirely on our own. It means none of us has a chance."

26

WHAT'S HAPPENED to the circuits of the moon? They've speeded up. They've left me behind. I'm not sure about the month, let alone the day, unless someone makes a point of saying "Sunday" or "Thursday." All I know is that I have Nuala and Brigit near me for twelve hours three or four days in a row, and then three or four days of emptiness.

Today is one of the gloomiest days I can remember. Low clouds amputate the tops of the tallest buildings in my view and swirl down their own gray tendrils along with the mist and the rain. It's Irish weather I think; Nuala knows about it. She also knows how you can spend hours watching the drops trickle down the window, staring at the watery traffic lights and the yellow taxis, gleaming in ways they never do in the sun. She's noticed the odd way people lean forward into the rain, like troops under fire move, feeling that the leaning will protect them. It's a reflex, they say.

But I'm lost in the mists and the gritty urban rain. I don't even know what time it is when Nuala and Brigit come in carrying a small package they've wrapped in red paper and tied with yellow ribbon. They hand it to me, smiling without a word. I tear it open with my claw—which is becoming more useful since Cindy started electrocuting me and the other Cindy built my brace—and my good right hand. It's a new Van Morrison CD. I smile and wave the disc toward my boom box. Nuala puts it on. It's perfect rain music, the sort of thing I'd listen to if I were painting, cozy in a cottage far from anywhere. I don't really know this since I've never been an artist, but it seems to me sad art must be much easier than happy art. If you look at what's been produced over the past few centuries, how many paintings in museums would you call "happy"?

"Congratulations," Nuala says. "You are far and away our prize now. This is your seventy-fifth day."

"I've never even had a boyfriend that long," Brigit says, kissing me on the cheek. "Nobody's ever lasted that long."

"You're too tough on them," Nuala says.

"But now we're ready to be rid of you," Brigit says. "We know you can't bear the idea of leaving us, but seventy-five days is really quite enough. It's the hospital record. So get better, will you? Or we'll just wheel you outside in a gurney one of these days and let you beg on the sidewalk."

Never happen, I mouth. You love me too much.

"Love or not, it's going to happen," says Nuala. "They've been watching your blood oxygen levels and how much pressure is coming from The Machine, and they think your diaphragm is now doing more than half the work. Pretty soon you'll be breathing on your own. Then you'll be off for a month with that little monster Cindy. She'll hurt you bad, until you run away from here on your own two feet."

"I'll be sad to see you go. I'll miss checking your catheter," Brigit says.

"God, Brigit," Nuala says.

"Well, I couldn't let Saint Nualala touch a man's privates now, could I? It wouldn't have been decent."

"Cindy's the one who'd like to get her hands on his privates," Nuala says. "You'd better be careful on her floor. You're not the sort who's into dominatrixes or anything, are you?"

Later the aides took me down the endless corridors to the CAT-scan station again. They used a hand pump instead of a canister of oxygen.

"You're breathing on your own," one of the aides said. "Look at this guy. I'm not pumping and his chest keeps rising and falling. Good sign for you, man."

It was a strange sort of breathing, not gasps exactly but the sort of quick snatches of breath I used to take when I was a kid on the swim team racing the breaststroke. The exhales were underwater and bubbled out powerfully, while the inhales were a fast large suck of air when my head broke water. Once I got the rhythm it wasn't bad, though I don't think I could have kept it up long. The aide let me try it for a few corridors and an eleva-tor ride and then started helping out with the pump. That was easier. But I felt elated to have done what I'd done. I was even cheerful to the CAT technicians as they slid me into their icy ci-gar tube and started the pinging and banging. I passed the time imagining myself in the not-too-distant future breathing all on my own. And that quickly broadened out into all sorts of wonderful possibilities: disconnection from the wet blue tubes of The Ma-chine, the lovely prospect of actually speaking to Nuala, a drink of orange juice, or better yet a cold Coke, a rare cheeseburger at the Bells, with fries and malt vinegar (or even just the hos-pital's Thursday night meatloaf, which was rumored to be excel-lent). This was all seeming quite heavenly as they pushed me back up to the ICU and plugged me back into the fentanyl and the antibiotics.

I WAS FLOATING in a private inner sea when Nuala came to check me out for the nightly handover. IVs all right, drips regular as can be, temperature a good ninety-nine, and The Machine doing its job but not laboring as hard as it used to; the wet voices in the blue tube were softer, less insistent. Nuala breathed on the head of her stethoscope, then held it between her palms to take off the chill before she listened to my heart and lungs. Her face was no more than six inches from mine, but her eyes were concentrated on her work.

When she'd finished, I gestured toward the stethoscope. She

leaned over me and placed the earphones in my ears. Then she
sat on the bed next to me and handed me the head. I blew on it
and handed it back to her. Then Nuala undid the middle button
of her white nurse's blouse and placed the head of the stethoscope
against the bare skin of her left breast, near the breastbone. At first
I heard nothing, and then suddenly my ears were full of the double
beat of her heart, the blood rushing smoothly in on one note and
rushing out on another. It was a strong, regular sound, lulling but
at the same time exciting. I was smiling, watching her face. She was
looking into my eyes.

I remembered a closeness from long ago.

The pace of the beating suddenly increased, and Nuala moved
the head of the stethoscope to that flat part of her chest above her
right breast. Now I couldn't hear the throb of her heart. Now I
heard her breathing, her lungs easily bringing in the air that life
depended on and easily expelling it again. It was a soft sound, a
beautiful sound, wavering, feathery.

I thought I heard the beating wings of some gentle bird.
There seemed to be softly beating wings all around me, carrying me away from the painful place. And I remember. What
Nuala had said about the dour men in the long woolen overcoats,
how they simply stand there and watch, and finally whisper to
you but never interfere. One could be standing just behind Nuala
now.

He hasn't any wings.

What would he whisper to me?

27

WHEN PEOPLE LEAVE the ICU for good, it's always a quiet affair. You never hear any screaming; you never know the pain of it. There's no fuss; there's no undue rush. A crew comes with a body bag; another crew comes to clean the room for the next victim.

They must spray something too because I always smell freesias. Nuala does as well. She tells me one day when a young woman is taken away, dead from meningitis. She says, "There was an Englishman who wrote 'The past is the only dead thing that smells sweet.' He died in nineteen-seventeen, not very old. Maybe he was in the Great War. He'd be an expert if he was a soldier. They say you could smell the trenches ten miles away."

She paused. "But he's not necessarily right, is he? For some people the past is never dead. You're one of those, I think. For me, my past reeks in my nostrils every day."

I WISHED the rest of the hospital had this discipline over death, this matter-of-factness. But that would have been giving up, wouldn't it? Surrendering. So at least once a day, the loudspeaker screams "Code ninety-nine, Schofield six. Code ninety-nine, Schofield six." It only takes you a few days to figure out that Code 99 means someone's heart has stopped. After the Code 99 is the location of the crisis. And instantly, faster than firemen, resuscitation experts rush to the scene. Everyone runs—doctors, nurses, technicians wheeling equipment. I saw this once when I was on my way downstairs for a CAT. We couldn't get around the crowd in the hall where the patient had dropped. I watched them slam on the oxygen. I watched them slap a paddle on either side of the patient's chest and jolt him until his hair stood straight up. They did this three times; then they took a needle of adrenaline that looked as big as a kitchen baster and plunged it into his heart. Still no pulse. No heartbeat. Nothing but a corpse. Those who had rushed to the scene walked quickly away, leaving the task of cleaning up to someone else.

The worst code, lying in your bed or sitting in your chair or even trying to walk to Cindy, was the quietest, it seemed. Although the volume of the loudspeakers never really changed. But there was a hush surrounding every "Code ninety-nine, Pediatrics. Code ninety-nine, Pediatrics." People always stopped whatever they were doing for a moment; people's eyes refused to meet. There was a moment of silence, instinctive but appropriate. Brigit told me less than five percent of Code 99 resuscitations were successful. Code 99, Pediatrics meant a dead child, another dead child. Twice I saw Nuala weep at a Code 99, Pediatrics.

There were never any Code 99s in the ICU. Here people's hearts stopped all the time, but it was expected, sometimes even a blessing. Everything necessary for an emergency resuscitation was on hand; there was no need for sprinting crews of specialists. If your heart stopped in the ICU, the staff just went quietly to work.

EXCEPT ONCE.

Except the most important once.

Except the one time that seasoned doctors and nurses panicked and someone sent a "Code ninety-nine, ICU, Code ninety-nine, ICU" screaming through the entire hospital.

Brigit went down, right in the corridor.

She was walking toward my end of the ward, carrying a tray of something, smiling brightly. And she just folded up like a puppet whose strings had suddenly been cut. She hit the floor hard, in a strange contorted heap. She went white instantly. Not even a finger twitched.

"Fentanyl, fentanyl!" Nuala was screaming as doctors wheeled up the machine and put the paddles on Brigit's chest. Her body jumped once and lay perfectly still. "It's a fentanyl OD, god-damn it," Nuala screamed. They tried the shocks again and again. "Narcan, she needs Narcan. Hurry, hurry, you fuck!" Nuala was punching one of the doctors in the arm again and again, begging for the one drug that could counter fentanyl ODs.

"Stop screaming about drugs! We've got a cardiac arrest here," the doctor shouted back as he plunged a useless hypo of adrenaline into Brigit.

"Oh, God, if it's fentanyl, she's fucked. Oh, fuck, Brigit. No, no."

Dr. Weinberg, head of the ICU, sprinted up as they rocked the body over and over with electricity.

"No!" he yelled, in sync with Nuala.

"Oh, fuck, oh, God, Brigit," he moaned. Then his head jerked up. "You! You dumb bastard!" he screamed at the baby-faced resi-dent who now seemed to be in shock. "Get me a hypo of Narcan. Now!"

The hypo was there in seconds. Dr. Weinberg stuck Brigit himself, tears running down his cheeks. She twitched once.

Too late. Brigit checked out. All the way out.

The medical team did not disperse this time, the way I had seen them do on the ninth floor. They stood around, shuffling, looking at poor little Brigit's corpse and the puddle of urine that was spreading out from where her hips lay on the hard floor. Nuala had her face to the wall and was sobbing violently. I was afraid she might collapse, her legs were trembling so hard. Nobody seemed able to move, or to leave, or to do anything at all for a while. No one spoke. But eventually they began to drift away, and the usual crew came for the corpse. Only Nuala and Dr. Weinberg stayed to watch them put a tag on Brigit's toe and zip her into a body bag. Weinberg had his arm around Nuala's shaking shoulders. The crew knew Nuala's and Weinberg's eyes were on them. They lifted this corpse with extra care and laid it gently on the gurney, almost as if it was a human being who could feel motion and pain.

After Brigit's Code 99, the staff psychologist was back. He wanted to be sure we could "reach closure" is how he put it as he pulled a chair up beside my bed. "How do you feel?" he asked. I motioned for him to hand me my alphabet board, which had only lost the Z when Brigit broke the corner off it. I wanted to spell FUCK YOU. FUCK YOUR CLOSURE. But instead I pointed to other letters and he wrote in his pad:

ANGELS HAVE LOST THEIR WINGS.

The psychologist smiled, gave me a look as if he understood and agreed, and left. I'm sure he thought I was doped up and didn't know a thing.

NUALA GOES ON LEAVE. She's gone for days. By looking exceptionally pitiful, I've gotten Patricia to photocopy my alphabet board about a hundred times. I want plenty of letters. I got her to find me a piece of cardboard about two feet square, some blunt-tipped children's scissors and some Elmer's glue. I cut out the letters and paste them on the cardboard, a little raggedly but as true as I could. I used the words from a sad German poem. And I lay there with this big cardboard note on my chest all night before the morning I knew Nuala was due back on duty. It said:

AND IF THE EARTHLY NO LONGER KNOWS YOUR NAME,

WHISPER TO THE SILENT EARTH: I'M FLOWING.

TO THE FLASHING WATER SAY: I AM.

BRIGIT FOREVER

I must have been napping when Nuala came in that morning. When I woke up I saw my sign neatly propped on the chair where I could read it from my bed. There was also a fresh tube in the IV in my left wrist, done so gently I never knew it had been replaced.

28

ONE AFTERNOON not long after Brigit died, when the world's turning slowed and the sun began its leisurely fall behind the Palisades of the Hudson, I suddenly felt it was wrong that the earth should still be spinning at all. Everything ought to have stopped the moment Brigit went down. How can anything ever be normal again? How can Cindy come into my room and expect me to rise from my bed and walk to her? How can Dr. Weinberg come to the ward each day? How can Nuala and Susan and Patricia go about their duties?

But we all go on. We walk away from Brigit. She's gone; we'll never see her again. And everything continues: The world revolves; people do their jobs. How long will Brigit last in the hearts of those who loved her? How long before she fades and disappears, as her body has done?

Ah, God.

There are holes in my life. Days and weeks and months are blank, have vanished completely in all detail. And not just the periods of my semi-comatose states. Huge pieces of my childhood, large slices of my adult life are gone. I'm losing myself bit by bit, just as I'm already losing Brigit.

In the silence of my room, I hear Nuala's voice. "You're the one who is knowing me too well. That's who you are right now," she says, tenderly. "I'm becoming afraid you won't like what you'll find, and you'll turn away from me. Please stop now."

I look around for her, but there is no one. I would do anything for Nuala, but I don't know what exactly to stop. Can I stop myself from dreaming of her, of her secrets? There's no answer, only the clockwork sound of the morphine drip. It's that quiet part of the day before the nursing shifts change and the residents make their brusque rounds.

Suddenly my heart rate picks up, but not enough to set off the alarm that would send the nurses sprinting to my side. My eyes start to roll back in my head. There's no reason for a coma; my signs have been fine all day. But I can feel my eyes roll, and it's frightening. I reach for the alarm button but miss it, and then I'm gone.

It's terrible. I'm inside a De Chirico painting, *The Anguish of Departure*. I can feel the texture of the ugly brown paint under my bare feet as I walk across a square with too much light and odd shadows. Off to the right is a white semiclassical building that gives off an unearthly aura. In the distance, in De Chirico's typically flat, unfeeling colors, is a colossal smokestack attached to nothing, no factory or plant. At that distance the train, billowing white steam, looks tiny and pointless, as if it could have no destination at all but still must leave the station at the appointed time, as trains did in De Chirico's Italy. I'm walking fast in the awful bright light but I don't seem to be getting any nearer the train. It's bound to leave any moment. I hear the whistle. Now I understand that I am in a painting that depicts everywhere and everyone who's ever left me behind. It's life as a continual good-bye that never includes a final kiss or embrace.

Where's my Brigit? Where is she?

That missing good-bye, that final failure, depresses me. Maybe they don't want to see me die, but I would like to have a final touch from Clare or from my brother. I would like one from Nuala. If I felt myself going, I decided, I would hold on any way I could until she came back to work. But would that be any good? I remembered my father. One moment we were talking about my wrestling match on Saturday; the next he was on the floor, his eyes wide open, staring at nothing, his heels pounding reflexively on the floor. Was that any kind of a good-bye? I was angry at him for a long time, as if dying had been his fault, something he could have chosen not to do.

I hope it was nothingness he was seeing as his heels drummed the floor. I hope it wasn't like the things I saw when I checked out. I hope to hell he wasn't seeing an aircraft hangar in the Nevada desert. He'd already been there once, during the war. I wouldn't wish it twice on anybody.

Does the fact of having lived entitle you to a satisfying good-bye? I doubt anyone is entitled to anything, although hard-luck cases like me always come around to thinking they're owed some kind of break. But I know I've already had mine; I've had Clare, close as blood, and I've had Brigit and Nuala. And a gash in the throat, a breathing tube, and scars up and down my chest don't seem like so much of a price anymore. I actually felt a little proud of my scars. They talked about plastic surgery to minimize them later on, but I laughed at the idea.

Scars are proof that you've lived some life. I wouldn't trust anyone with no scars. Nuala was prettier for the little raised white cicatrix above her left eye (from a bang by a curragh oar when she was six or so).

THEN MY EYES ROLL FORWARD. I see Nuala, her lips white and jaw muscles clenched, taking my pulse. "Oh, Jesus, here you are," she says when she sees I'm looking at her. "Why do you scare me like that? I thought I was losing you again. Any pain? Feeling unusual?" I make the circling sign for crazy next to my temple.

I see Nuala is wearing an Ace bandage on her left ankle.

Friday, I mouth.

"Sure is. How did you know?" she asks. I point to her bandage.

"Ah, the detective at work. You know I go bowling on Thursday, cool people and punks' night at the Village lanes. You figure I twisted my ankle, probably trying to use a ball that was too heavy for me to impress someone or other. You see the bandage. You draw your conclusions." She's smiling happily at me now.

I nod.

"What else have you figured out?" she asks.

Due respect, no underpants today, I mouth.

"Christ on a crutch! How would you know a thing like that? That pisses me off."

Sorry. Small tear in skirt. Whole ward see your ass. No clean ones this morning, right?

"Yeah. I forgot to do the laundry. Just like Brigit. God bless her and keep her. But this kind of thing feels a little too intimate. I think you should keep your detective work to yourself."

No work. Obvious. See your ass.

"You are getting crazier. I'm going to tell the doctors to lay off the morphine for a while, see if that makes you behave."

Nuala?

"What now? I've got to go sew this skirt and get to work.

Sweet ass.

"Flip bastard," she said, leaving.

Later on the pulmonary specialist comes by, carrying whole wads of X rays. He doesn't want to use the board or even try to read my lips. He just wants to tell me things. It seems everything in my lungs is clearing up nicely except that damn lower right lobe.

"Now that's a problem. We've got to keep that one really clean, so you're going to get some new antibiotics. The reason's simple: If it gets infected badly again, I'm afraid we won't just be able to tube you. We'll finally have to do a full operation and cut the thing out. And we're not sure you'd survive general anesthesia. Understand?"

I nod.

He gives me the thumbs-up. "But that's just a worst case. I personally think your lungs are going to clear up, and your diaphragm is working better every day. Maybe soon we can get you off that tube and into a mask. We'll see. Just keep hanging in there."

I don't even try to ask about odds. He wouldn't tell me. They think optimism is good homeopathy, though most of them haven't much use for the rest of that stuff.

NUALA SHOCKS ME THAT NIGHT. She comes by after she's gone off duty, wearing tight leather jeans and her motorcycle boots. Her legs look much longer than you'd think for someone who's just five-foot-five. It must be the boots. And I bet she doesn't weigh more than a hundred pounds without them. She looks about eighteen in the soft light of my room. I've got my opera sopranos on the boom box.

"Sorry I got cross with you this morning. It would have been embarrassing going around all day with my ass hanging out, not even knowing it. Actually"—she laughs—"most of the patients probably wouldn't have noticed. But those goddamn horny interns would've."

She's quiet for a while, watching the lights go on over the city. "Sinead's fine in case you were wondering. She's getting huge though. I'm going to have to put her on a diet."

Then she starts to cry. "How could I have let Brigit get that far? I should have stopped it."

I shake my head no.

"I could have stopped it," she insisted.

Can't save people who made up their minds, I mouth.

"People who've what?"

Made up their minds.

"You think she meant to kill herself? That's crazy. Not Brigit. She loved life."

Only risks. Took one too many. Didn't mean to go. Not that way.

"When, then? How?"

Years and years. Alcohol or drugs.

"But she was a happy girl."

Lived for fun. All for fun. Sooner, later, fun runs out. Empty. Not yet, but would have come. Brigit knew. Just got timing all wrong.

Nuala was struggling to understand me. She had her face within inches of my mouth so she could hear the hisses I could make as well as see my lips. I wanted her to see that no one thought it was her fault, no one was blaming her. She wasn't, after all, responsible for what Brigit snuck around doing. Nuala had no real way of stopping her.

Not your fault. Never your fault, I mouthed.

"But I'll dream it was forever," Nuala said. "I'll see Brigit crumpled on that floor for the rest of my life."

Bad dreams fade, I mouthed.

But the good nights lead to the worst days anyway, I want to tell her, but can't. The dreams I have now are as depressing as death. I dream I can run for miles like a Masai warrior, with wind to spare. I dream I can play a fast game of tennis, ski black diamonds, make 1,000-meter vertical ascents in the Dolomites.

And sometimes I dream I can fly. I'm soaring on the updrafts, and suddenly I dive and skim the contours of the ground like a falcon, moving so fast the world below me's a blur.

And on specially good nights, I dream I am making slow tender love, with the one single person that I love.

Always wake up in this broken body, I mouthed. No life, no love. Real bad dream.

Nuala said, "You'll live and love. The only problem with love is knowing when you find the right one."

Easy, I mouthed.

"For you, maybe. I'm always so unsure. How far do I trust a man or my own instincts? I've made so many mistakes I've just about given up."

Never quit. Learned that from Brigit, you.

"I've been lying," Nuala said. "Sometimes I feel like I deserve to be back in the well, with all the other croakers."

————

BACK IN THE WELL. An ugly town on a beautiful bay, a town that got nothing from the oil money—beyond a few jobs for a while and some hideous mercury vapor street lights. Now the men allow themselves to think their dead pasts smell sweet, and the mercury lights glare harshly over the shuttered houses and the one or two pubs still open. At night, from a distance, the town looks like an angry boil, inflamed against the black hills behind it. People don't sleep as soundly as they used to because of the glaring lights. Boys with slingshots try to shoot them out sometimes, but the glass is too thick, much thicker than car headlights, their second targets of choice.

"People give up at an early age in Ireland," Nuala is saying. "They're old and settled in their twenties. They're resigned. The only things that would upset them are if the pub closed or the telly failed during a big football match."

Why you so different? I mouth.

"I've never known. Born into a clear sun, maybe. Maybe because my grandfather let me name his boat Blue Johnny. Maybe because my parents saw the future and sent me to nursing school in Dublin to escape it. I never had the chance to settle for the dead old ways, thanks to them. Maybe it's never been me at all who's different, but them. Maybe that's why I never mind the begging letters.

" 'Course, I changed too, like anyone else. The big one for me was my grandda dying. We had a lovely old-fashioned funeral for him, all the village walking behind the hearse drawn by two black ponies with stiff cockades rising between their ears. The men wore their cheap black suits and shoes that probably wouldn't survive more than one or two funerals or weddings in the rain. And the rain it did rain down that day.

"I slipped out after the burial to go to the shingle where Blue Johnny was beached. It took all my strength to get it afloat. But I did, and I rowed it to one of my grandda's favorite fishing spots. Then I chopped a hole in the bottom with a hatchet and sat there until it was awash and sure to sink. Then I swam for the rocks, nearly drowned by the pull of my long black dress. When I walked back into the wake an hour or so later, everyone was too drunk to notice my condition. They thought I'd just been for a stroll in the rain.

"Two weeks later I left for Dublin, with my fiberboard suitcase, a crucifix 'round me neck, and the address of the nursing school on three pieces of paper: one in my mackintosh pocket, one in my blouse pocket, and one in the suitcase. It felt like insurance that I'd never get lost."

DUBLIN DAYS. Brigit and Nuala, Nuala and Brigit, spending their hours in a sprawling, turreted Victorian monstrosity called St. Agnes College of Nursing. All damp red brick, moss in the mortar, and gritty black wrought-iron banisters on the stairways. Windows with a century of grime on the outside no amount of scrubbing seemed able to remove. Dank and underheated in the winter. Scarred wooden desks in the classrooms and chipped white enamel tables in the laboratories. Teachers (nuns, of course) rustling down the long, high corridors like ghosts.

But the instruction is excellent. Many of the nuns have practiced nursing in wild, faraway places where the nearest hospital might be two or three days away by bullock cart or riverboat. They did the work of doctors in these outposts; they acquired knowledge far beyond what a modern hospital nurse might have. This is what they are trying to pass on to a generation of girls who've sometimes dyed their hair odd colors, had various parts of their bodies pierced, or even acquired tattoos in intimate places.

They begin at the beginning: taking temperatures and pulse rates, cleaning wounds, applying antiseptics and sterile bandages. They learn to fluff pillows and turn immobile patients on their sides from time to time, so bedsores won't develop. They perfect the delicate art of slipping a bedpan beneath a bed-ridden patient and removing it without spilling. They learn to find veins and gently slip in the thin, sharp points of hypodermics. They learn to take blood, to regulate intravenous drips so the patients get neither too much nor too little of whatever it is they need. Toward the end they learn the almost mystical skill of diagnosis. Of reading the lights and graphs of various monitors, of judging conditions from the colors of fingernails and skin, and how the flesh responds when pressed, and how the breath smells and the eyes dilate.

As for everything else, Brigit led the way. She was Nuala's roommate. And Nuala covered for her when she snuck out alley-catting, which she usually did on Thursday nights, figuring the housemother would not be so vigilant as she might on Fridays or

Saturdays. Brigit had started a year before Nuala, and when she finished went immediately to New York, where the big hospitals were recruiting. Nuala's last year at school was lonely. Then her time came to take the train from Dublin to Shannon and board an Aer Lingus flight to New York. Brigit was there to meet the plane, to put Nuala up in her apartment, to take her for an interview at her hospital.

"Wherever I turned," Nuala says, "there was Brigit, looking out for me.

"My bright Brigit, the best insurance of all against anything going wrong. The only insurance I ever had."

29

WE'RE WALKING AWAY. I make the five steps to
Cindy. She's smiling at me like a welcoming lover.
Then the perky bitch steps back a yard. "I dare you!"
she says.

My arms are trembling; I can't keep them still.
Those red hot rods are burning down the backs of
my legs. I look hard at her until the smile goes out of
her eyes, and then I take three quick steps dead at her,
attacking. She has to step back. Then my arms give
out and the hot rods force my legs to bend away from
the pain.

But she's there, quick as a ferret, kicking the
walker out of the way, catching me as I go down. I
can see her breasts press against me, looking down the

loose collar of her sweatshirt. Cover 'em up, I mouth. Don't need any flashers here.

She starts to laugh and nearly drops me, but between her and Nuala they get me back to my bed. The absence of pain, once I'm lying there, is more overwhelming than the pain itself had been. "You're trouble, mister. We're going to have to restrain you soon to keep you from chasing us around the Unit," Cindy says. She's got that merry look back in her black eyes.

Although the ICU is nearly empty and various nurses filling in for Brigit help make Nuala's work load fairly light, she seldom visits my room during her shift. She leaves me to the others. It's in the evenings, when she's off duty, that she comes to sit. She sometimes stays for an hour even, just talking about this and that.

I get to see her out of those starchy white uniforms, and I love the way she dresses. She wears short knit skirts or short leather skirts, usually black or deepest green, and soft knit sweaters of the same color—sometimes baggy cable-knits and sometimes tight merinos or cashmeres. She wears dark, heavy tights against the late spring chills, and her motorcycle boots of course; she's saving the little Italian flats for something special. And sometimes her hair is free, a great reddish cloud around her small face.

I think perhaps some miracle has happened, perhaps she's a little in love with me. Or maybe she's just lonely now that Brigit's gone; no companion for the Bells of Hell. I tell her I'll take her there as soon as they unplug me; I'll travel by wheelchair.

"Never again," she says. "Not without Brigit. That damn place is haunted for me."

Somewhere new, then. Tribeca or the Lower East Side. I'll take you.

"That may not be so long," she says. "Your diaphragm's doing more work every day. And your blood counts are getting much better, your fevers fewer. You seem to've turned the corner. You might be a human being again, if we can do something about that hair." It hasn't been cut since I got here.

The next day Nuala gets the hospital barber to give me a trim. Not quite Marine short, but a lot tighter than the wild matted mess I had after three months in bed, with never a proper shampoo or a shower.

Nuala shrieks when she sees it. "Jesus, now you do look like a cop. And not from the art squad either. You look like a motorcycle cop in a bad mood. Like you're giving me a ticket even though I'm cute." I try laughing out loud but it fucks up the flow from the blue tube.

"So, what do you want to know about me?" Nuala asks one evening not long after my haircut.

Everything, I mouth emphatically.

"Do you want to know my pathetic story? I know you were always asking Brigit, God rest her. She never told you about Robbie, did she?"

Never, I swear.

"She never gave out my secrets, did she?"

Never ratted, even when asked police-type questions.

"Then how did you know about Robbie? You were in a coma . . ."

You told me, I mouthed. You were in there with me. Truly.

"Not in a million years," she said. "Just another hallucination. I doubt you've had a hallucination-free day since you've been here. Besides everything else, you've been getting enough drugs to kill Brigit five times over. You're indestructible. But a little crazy."

Sure, Nuala, I thought, *that's nice.*

Earlier in the day my primary physician had dropped by. It was my eighty-something day there, an impossible stay. He said, "I'm going to be straight with you. We've tried everything we medically know how to do. And there's been some improvement lately. But there's nothing left for us to try if you have another crisis. We can maintain you. We can't pull you back if you go over the edge though. I don't like to say it, but you deserve the truth. The odds aren't good. It's practically out of our hands. It's up to you. If your diaphragm finally starts working normally, and if you can escape another infection, you'll make it."

It shook me. Even though people were dying all around me every day, I had the feeling that I was just under a prolonged siege. I saw my death, but I thought that they'd always pull me through, that there was always something new to pump into my veins. I never really imagined we'd reach the point where medicine might no longer work. I spent most of the afternoon staring at the damn clock. I was furious, raging at myself. It was so logical that it had never really crossed my mind. One day they'd reach the last combination of antibiotics. And if there were something resistant to that (which they couldn't know), well, that would be it.

I started getting anxious each evening when the aide came to take my temperature. Anything under 100 was a relief. They didn't consider anything under 100 a fever, and as long as I had no fever I knew I was going to wake up the next morning. At least I thought I knew. This evening I'd been 99.7; safe enough but not as comforting as 98.6.

"SO YOU'RE LUCID NOW—here's my tale," Nuala says. It's getting dim in the room but neither of us can stand the fluorescents. We have October Project on softly, sad melodies in the background muting the mechanical noises of The Machine.

"When I came to New York, I wasn't wild at all. Brigit was already rolling, but I couldn't be coaxed. I was too serious about my career, about making a life for myself. Mostly I worked. I volunteered to fill in for absentees. I did overtime when it was needed, things like that.

"Outside the hospital, I went wherever Brigit and her crowd took me. After a while I met some boys, had some affairs—you know, for a month or two. Those ones that start with sparks. You must have had your share of those. No wife, at your age. You must have been a difficult one."

In love once, in my twenties. She left me. You know that, I mouth. Never met right one after. Maybe waiting for you.

"Don't say that," she said. Then she just stared out the window for a while.

"I wasn't expecting anything when I met Robbie," she suddenly continued. "He was a nice American, a year younger than me. He worked at an advertising agency, doing artwork on the Macs. A nice clean boy with manners and kindness, who would try hard to understand me even when I was being difficult. 'Keep hold of him,' Brigit kept saying. 'He's a rare one.' She'd have known. She'd been around the block.

"And something special started. After about six months, I started thinking about the future, moving in together maybe. He seemed to think my thoughts sometimes. A few times I think we shared the same dreams, literally, the ones you have at night.

"I would go to his house every day after work. He'd have something nice cooking for supper, and when I was tired he didn't mind. I'd just sit, and he'd massage my shoulders and my feet. I loved soaking in his tub—he had one of those deep old ones with feet—and then eating dinner wearing his flannel bathrobe. It was so perfect, so much what I needed. He was always tender. He let me have my silences. He never pried.

"One Saturday in January, he woke up with a bad cough and a fever. I kept him in bed, gave him aspirin and fluids. Sunday the cough was thicker, the fever up to one-oh-two. Monday it hit one-oh-three; and he was wheezing with each breath. So I took him to the emergency room. They checked him in, IV'd him, put an oxygen mask on his face. He was very frightened; he'd never been so sick. I stayed with him all day, held his hand, talked to him of the things we'd do when he was better. Then the doctor came in, not one I really knew. He took me out into the corridor. 'The sputum tests show Pneumocystis carinii pneumonia. Get his permission.'

"I thought my heart would leave my throat. I had to explain to Robbie why the usual antibiotics weren't helping him much. He agreed to the test, I think because he didn't believe it was possible. How could he have AIDS? I could see that question in his eyes."

Nuala begins weeping uncontrollably.

"He even asked if it was possible I'd gotten it at the hospital and carried it home to him."

Slowly the weeping subsides. I can see what it's costing her to regain control. The pain doesn't leave her face; her jaws are tight, her lips pale.

"The test was positive, of course," she says. "So they did a second one.

"He was dead in a week.

"My world broke into pieces so small it seemed like I'd never even been born. I got tested immediately: HIV-negative. But it wasn't enough for me. Every month for almost two years I've had the test again, and every time it's HIV-negative."

Nuala bows her head in her hands and sobs quietly for a few minutes. "For weeks after Robbie died, I went to bed every night wearing this black cashmere turtleneck I'd given him for Christmas. He'd never even worn it, because he said it was too beautiful for the office. I wore it and wore it, so many nights that it pilled all over and began to smell. So I threw it away finally. Off the Staten Island Ferry, into the water."

Then she says, "I found out that Robbie had sometimes shot up coke. It was a dirty needle that got him. Had to be. I hate him for it still, and always will. I love him and always will. But I feel tainted, like I'm carrying the infection around in my womb. Like I'm pregnant with death. I can't love anyone. I'll only kill them.

"I've seen so many shrinks; they all say it's absurd. I know I'm fine. But the feeling of being a carrier won't leave me. I can't stand it. I need to be free of it."

Nuala pauses. "So you got it right. I don't know how you heard it. I don't know what goes on in your comas. Maybe Brigit did let it slip."

I wanted to get out of bed and take her in my arms. I try to, and the blue tube pulls away from my throat. Nuala puts it back. I take her hand and kiss it. I just hold it against my mouth, moving my lips against her palm, trying to tell her things I have no words for. I manage to get my left arm around her waist. She pulls away gently, but I hold her. I put my good hand where her wings ought to have been. I whisper against her palm: Nuala you are pure and perfect, pure and perfect.

But see the world I'm in with Nuala. A dying man clasping her, a wreck of a man with no future, obsessed with a future with her, a crying man whispering silently into her palm. Nuala stands dry-eyed, wondering what to believe and thinking that if she believes anything, all she faces is another heartbreak. Or maybe she feels nothing but the relief of a confession to a person who will soon pass from her life.

Who can know? Perhaps it doesn't matter, at the end of the day. I wouldn't want to be the judge of that, though.

CINDY WITH THE adorable tits comes back every other day now. I notice today, though, that she's wearing a bra under her sweatshirt, and I can make her blush just by catching her eye in the right way. She starts me at six steps now and doesn't do the stepping back at the last one trick. At the end of a week, we've advanced to seven. She says it's a great improvement, but I'm skeptical. I still can't get out of the bed by myself. I can't wheel myself into the bathroom, and on those few occasions when I've been helped to make it there, I've been so stiff I couldn't wipe myself. You'll never know how flexible you have to be just to wipe your own ass until you've spent three months in bed and lost it all. And I was gasping for air by the time I got back to bed and they plugged me into The Machine.

But I've lucked out. Nuala's new partner is Patricia. She's gangly, full of friendship. So I try to save up certain bodily needs for when she's around. I don't want Nuala to see me more than she has to. I don't want her to have to wipe my ass. I prefer her to watch me struggling on my walker—some evidence of my gaining strength—toward Cindy, who sometimes leaps over the damn thing in sheer excess of energy and health. She irritates the hell out of me.

My temperature stays below 100 for a week. They've started

unhooking my blue tube for fifteen minutes or so several times a day to see how I'm breathing on my own. Not too bad. They give me a glass of orange juice to see if I can swallow without getting anything into my lungs. I hate orange juice. But I have never tasted anything better. It is the first liquid to enter my mouth in three months. The sensation of swallowing something wet is paradisiacal. I do OK. The next day they try me on a yogurt. That's good too. The tubes are taken out of my chest one by one. They start to seriously wean me from the morphine. I feel cranky and out of my head the first couple of days, but then a clearness comes over my mind that I can scarcely remember having before. I feel very hopeful, as if maybe I'll be one of the lucky ones who leaves with his brain intact.

One day Nuala helps me into a wheelchair, and I'm taken by an aide to a lab deep in the basement where I've never been before. In front of a huge machine made of thick Plexiglas tubing and various valves, a mask is strapped to my face. A doctor explains that we're checking my lung capacity. I'm simply to follow his instructions. Suddenly he's shouting like a football coach, "Blow! Blow! Blow! Keep it coming! Blow! Blow!" A graph comes chattering out of the machine. He rips it off and puts it into a file. "Now, the other way, he says, and he's screaming, "Inhale! That's it, suck it in. Inhale! Inhale!" Another graph comes chattering. "Not too bad. About fifty percent of predicted capacity," he says and wheels me out into the corridor. I sit there for fifteen minutes waiting for an aide to take me back upstairs. I feel exhausted. I know I didn't do well on the blowing. My lungs just won't fill with air. It's agony to sit there. There's so little flesh to cushion the bones.

A FEW NIGHTS LATER, just before they pass out the sleeping pills and give the hypos, a crew comes pushing a gurney into the room next to mine. I see a filthy figure with a sweating feverish face. Two nurses begin to undress him before transferring him to the bed. All at once they run screaming from the room. "Lice! He's got lice!" one of the Filipinas is shouting. He's one of the street people the hospital ambulances sometimes pick up; the nurses call them "skeletons." They never last long. Some orderlies wheel him away, and an hour later he's back in a clean gown and put into his bed. He's got an oxygen tube going down his throat and a couple of IVs. He's out of it, I can see that. I'm a veteran.

He dies after a day and most of a night, just before dawn.

Two days later my temperature shoots up to 103, and they accuse me of fighting The Machine. They're going to paralyze me again. "Goddamn fucking staph again," I hear one of the third-year residents say. "Shit. The skeleton was probably radiating the stuff."

But things are not too clear when you're up around 103 or more. I feel Nuala hovering but I can't make out what she's up to. They ram a steel drainage tube into one of my old barely closed chest holes. I get a big hit of fentanyl. There's a brief period of euphoria. I think I can hear myself saying, "Nuala, let's go dancing. Let's go to Indochine and then go dancing." But no one can hear me.

Still, I hear Nuala say, "Sure, love to go. Let me just get changed."

I hear Patricia say, "His pulse is up to one-thirty already." I'm feeling that fentanyl euphoria that killed Brigit. *Not going to kill me*, I think. I get just enough. But my vision is getting blurry. I realize I am crying. "Are you in pain?" Patricia asks.

I shake my head no. This isn't pain, even with that steel tube. This is a picnic. Pain is what happens when your eyes roll back in your head. You fight to bring them back into focus; you fight to keep them in the middle where you can see. But the instant you stop concentrating on holding them there, they roll again. They want so much to look into your head, to see the red darkness in there. Or maybe to see the enemy, the tiny creatures that are destroying you. Pain is when you know you can't stop the rolling, when you know you're checking out—for the third or fourth or maybe fifth time.

"Oh, fuck," the resident says as I go. "We've lost him again."

30

THE WILD PONIES stand with their tails to the salty wind. Their bones are heavy and raw, their haunches angular. They're evil and sullen as the thin nags of death in a Dürer etching. They're motionless. Their great heads seem too weighty for their necks; their muzzles are hanging inches from the damp grass. They are a greasy ash gray. They've never once been brushed or groomed. They snort irritably at each other, their eyes as dull and cold and implacable as the northern sea beside which they live.

We are on a barrier island along the Atlantic coast. From the other side of the tall dunes, I can hear the hiss and boom of a heavy surf. There's the taste of salt on my lips. Where we are, the runnels and channels of a marsh run blackly around tussocks of yellow and green grass, among islands of some low-creeping cedar. You cannot tell how deep the black water is: a foot or a mile. I see a blue heron stepping delicately around a little mound of grass, as if it is ashamed that each poised foot must break the glassy surface of the water and descend into the mud before the next step can be taken. It is the most sinister bird in the world, this beautiful delicate stalker whose only purpose is to surprise and spear some small fish.

We're here for something larger. There are six Indians with me. They all look like degraded versions of that classic face on the old buffalo nickel. They are wearing bright yellow oilskin coats, black rubber pants, and black rubber boots. They don't have any weapons. They're speaking a language I've never heard, but I understand everything they say, as if the words are going directly to the center of my brain where ideas beyond words are processed. There are two canoes in the black water. We climb into them and start to paddle down the channels. As we glide along, there is the strange frightening sense of passing over an abyss, followed by relief when it seems the black water is shallow again. A light rain begins to pock the waters. The Indians have pulled up their hoods; I can no longer tell who is speaking. The marsh is utterly flat; except for the tussocks and small islands of grass, there are only the sickly yellow dunes behind us to the east and the dark ominous scrawl of a forest's edge miles to the west. No birds fly across the whole vast gray globe of sky. There is only the hiss of the wind, the squeak of rubber coats, the dripping paddles.

I feel I am at the last place on earth, and it is empty.

I trust the Indians will not hurt me, but may by the power of their will end my life this day, if they feel it is right to do so.

They are saying that the next creature lives in this marsh, the creature beyond man. They are saying that it has the exact shape of man but has no ears. It has webbing between its fingers and toes. It is pale, like a white man, it swims underwater like a man swims, and it climbs out of the water and walks. If you approach it, it will silently send ideas inside your head, which you will understand. You have no need to speak. It will understand all your ideas in turn. But you feel you are talking to an elder, a man of superior knowledge. This creature lives equally in the water and on the land. The usual rules of life do not apply to it. There is no thought you can have that it does not understand; there is no idea of yours that it does not anticipate. It knows the answers to all questions.

But it will not simply give them on demand.

The Indians are saying I am meant to join this creature's family—that I've been chosen, which is why I have appeared among them. I must, at the right spot, dive down into the black water until I can hold my breath no longer. Until my burning lungs suck in the water. But these creatures will not let me drown. They will gather me in their arms and breathe into my mouth and make me one of them. I will live in the watery world. And I will know everything in the universe, how it was born, what it means, the secret of life and death—that there is no difference between them except the one we make in our minds.

Every one of the Indians says he hopes to be chosen someday but doubts the privilege will come to him.

I watch the thin smudge of forest on the horizon. I search the black waters over which we are gliding. There is nothing to be seen but my own dull reflection. The rain is more insistent now and chilly.

Is this a chance at a new life, at some kind of immortality, or just a grotesque annihilation? If this is the next evolutionary stage, the next spiritual level, why has it been revealed only to these Indians? I am terribly frightened of the black water: Even in warm tropical seas, all light fades into absolute darkness if you dive deep enough. And the cold, the bone-cracking cold, everlasting and without change—this is the realm of no weather, no sunshowers or rain, no clouds, no wind or motion at all. There could be a hurricane above and no sign of it at all down there. It's perfect stasis. It's a dead man's world, the deep.

I don't want this, now or ever. It cannot be my time. I want Nuala's warmth, Nuala's presence.

I say no.

I say I must go back at once.

The Indians give no sign that they've heard me. But in unison they switch their paddles to the other sides of the canoes. Soon we glide out of the marsh and into the stretch of open water toward the forest. The canoes buck in the rougher water; they skid over whitecaps, their tails twisting sideways. The Indians know how to handle this. When we reach the shore, I have to walk through a few feet of water to the sand. They don't acknowledge my departure. They paddle back toward the marsh and vanish in the fog that is now rolling over the dunes in dense weightless waves.

From where I have been put ashore, I walk a mile or so through dripping loblolly pines to a highway. Some distance to the south there is a huge steel bridge, crossing waters I cannot see an end to because of the mist and rain. There's a dock; maybe there will be a ferry.

Then I am in a room at a motel beside the ferry dock. It's late. A big wall clock in my room has hands and numbers that glow, like the clocks they used to have in diners. I'm lying there in a double bed, watching the clock and the reflected flash of the red and green lights revolving on posts at the end of the dock. It's after midnight. I feel I should make a phone call, but I don't know whom to call. I think the ferry will come soon to take me away from this place, but I'm frightened to find I have no wallet in my pants pockets, nothing in my shirt, no bags, not even any shoes or socks. I won't be able to buy a ticket. I will have to lie here watching the glowing clock and the red and green lights forever. Ferry after ferry after ferry will come and I will be left behind, unable to rise from this bed.

I begin thinking of the ones I've lost. Not just my grandfather, my father; but Allen, who died at thirty of leukemia; Kevin, who shot himself at thirty-two; Rick, who was crushed in a car wreck at twenty-nine; Dempsey, who had a brain disease so rare I don't think it had a name; Dick, by a VC mine; Carlo, by lung cancer; Gus, by a heart attack; Maria, by a blood clot that traveled from her leg to her heart two days after she gave birth to a healthy girl. And the man I killed without meaning to, when I was a rookie cop.

And not just the ones lost to death. I think of all the girls I slept with who might have been friends if I'd behaved differently, the men at work who could've been friends if I'd met them halfway, the smiling stranger to whom I would not speak and thus would never know, and Clare, most of all Clare, who possessed a small piece of my soul.

Nuala always says Robbie was murdered. He died of a disease, but to Nuala, AIDS isn't a disease. It's a stone-cold killer, like the crack kid on the street who pulls out a 9mm and shoots you in the head because you've somehow violated his stupid and obscure code of respect. He'll stand amazed at the way blood and brains splatter everywhere, because he never really imagined what happens when a bullet pierces a skull.

Nature seems crazy now, like the kid with the 9mm. More senseless than ever, getting better armed: Ebola, Marburg, TB that shrugs off drugs, unknown killers, lurking, waiting for their time.

Are the Indians out there paddling still, looking for the creature in the depthless black channels of the marsh? What does it mean if such a creature exists—more intelligent, with no need of cities and Machines, with the answers to everything in the universe born into its mind?

Have we only been dreaming ourselves all along?

I smell the salt air. It's chilly and seems to lie heavily in my lungs. The sheets are clean but gritty and damp. My limbs are stiff. I can't sit up. I must lie there and endure, and it will always be night, with a glowing clock that measures only the failure of time to release me.

"Don't worry about the ferry," a voice says. "You don't need the ferry." The voice belongs to someone I watched drop like a puppet, someone I saw in a body bag. I start to tremble.

I dread this dense, heavy night.

"Come on, buster. Come on. This is nothing you can't handle. You've been here before."

31

I'M IN A WORLD of wavering shades, shadowy figures. The blackness is no longer absolute, but I can't see any light. I sense vague forms above me. I think I hear things. There's a man's voice I can't recognize.

"Multiple episodes of acute pneumothorax. Count the drainage scars. He's had severe septicemia. He's been in and out of comas, and he's had fevers above one-oh-four, swelling of the spinal cord and brain. And there's the polyneuropathy.

"His lungs are as fragile as wet tissue paper. His liver or kidneys could give out any minute. Even if we can keep the oxygen levels up with the ventilator without rupturing his lungs, he can't last. I give him forty-eight hours."

Who is he talking about?

"It's all over, Nuala. You did your best. Just keep him comfortable with the morphine drip. OK?"

"Yes." It's Nuala's voice answering. Then I hear footsteps and, very near, a muffled sound like crying. Maybe it is just The Machine wheezing damply. But I'm almost sure I feel someone take my right hand and kiss it.

The crying sound increases. But then it stops.

I blink. Some time passes.

I blink again, then open my eyes.

There is some faint light in my room, a sort of glowing lucency. Everything feels provisional. There's a murmurous electrical humming in my brain. Things begin to look sharp, focused, but almost immediately everything is blurring at the edges. It's like an underwater world; there's a feeling of things in motion while I alone am absolutely still.

Then I see Nuala looking at me as though something disturbing has happened to my face. "Do you feel OK?" she's saying. "Do you feel strange in any way?" I can't seem to shake my head yes or no. Her voice sounds hollow, not like Nuala at all. For a moment I don't know where I am, and my pulse races. I feel I'm burning up from the inside out, like an old tree struck by lightning deep in its trunk. I am only dreaming Nuala, I think. Then I see my familiar things, my boom box and my broken alphabet board and Cindy's walker. Enya is playing. Nuala knows that music eases me. Nuala puts a tiny piece of ice in my parched mouth.

The light's dim but growing opalescent as a dawn. These are not the graying colors of dusk. I feel that I won't see those again.

Nuala has arranged the IV stands so she could put her chair as close as possible to the head of my bed. Did she sit with me all night? How many nights has it been? Did she hold my hand? Did she close her eyes and dream me back? Or did she just watch me, hour after hour? Her shift won't start for a long time yet.

She's very close to me. She never wears perfume but always has a faint sweet aroma around her hair. Her eyes are starting to catch and reflect the glow of the new day's light.

"Can you hear me? Do you know me? Do you know where we are now?"

She lilts and flashes. I can mouth, Yes. But it isn't certain. Is this really my room? Why do I feel I've crossed a certain barrier I can never pass back through?

"Then now we're going to talk at last." She reaches across my chest, smoothly unhooks The Machine's blue tube from my throat, and lets it drop. Panic seizes me, but my chest keeps rising and falling, moving flows of real air. I'm breathing. It's rough and raspy and feels insufficient. But I am doing it.

"I'll be soft with you. Don't be afraid."

She takes her right forefinger and blocks the gaping hole at the base of my throat where the tube has been connected all these months. I can feel the smooth, warm skin of her finger against the flaps of flesh around the wound. And then she's inside me.

This must be what it feels like for a woman to be penetrated, I think. This silky intrusion that frightens a little. My body stiffens.

"Just breathe through your nose, slowly, you can do it," Nuala says. "That's good, that's lovely, soft and slow. Now see if you can say something."

"Nuala," I say. The voice is croaking and hoarse, but the voice is mine. I hear that one word come from my dry mouth. It seems like a miracle.

She smiles. "Surely after three months you can think of something more important to say."

"Love," I croak.

"Tell me something real. Say what's going on in your mind."

"I feel so light. I can see through myself now. I'm almost transparent," I say.

"No, you're not, you're not. I can see you clearly," Nuala says. "You're here with me. Tell me your deepest feeling."

All the sense left in my wasted body is concentrated on the touch of Nuala's finger in my throat. "I feel we're lovers," I say.

"We are," Nuala says. "This is making love. It's beautiful. Do you love me as much as I love you? Will you always?"

Always? I remember an old Irish lament. I would like to sing it for her. But that's far beyond what I might manage. The air seems thinner, my breath shorter. So I chant:

"The sea is wide,
And I can't swim over,
And neither have I wings to fly.
I wish I could find me a handy boatman,
To ferry me over
To my love, and die."

No tears from Nuala, only her great green eyes on mine, only her soft finger alive in my throat. My eyelids are stiffening; I can't even blink. My body seems numb, except where Nuala is inside me.

She's dimming now, this glimmering girl. I can just feel one of her fingers tracing the black characters of my Chinese tattoo.

"Nuala," I whisper. " 'The soul in winter dreams. . . .' "

And from my Nuala comes one clear, strong reply: "I am your rising sun. Carry me with you."

AUTHOR'S NOTE

Bruno Vogrig, to whom this novel is dedicated, was a friend—almost a father to me, in fact—who survived combat in World War II and two years in a German concentration camp. He was an accomplished violinist, but circumstances never allowed him to pursue his art. Yet he was never bitter, for he had a perspective on life most of us never achieve. And he used to gently chide me whenever I'd complain about anything that was going wrong in my career or life.

"You never know," Bruno'd say, "what Signore Destino has in mind."

He was right, of course. While I worried about the irritations of daily life, I never suspected the destiny awaiting me: that a minor childhood disease would put me into a hospital for 5 months, with only a 5 percent chance of survival, and then into a year of physical therapy afterward, to learn how to walk and use my hands again.

The facts are simple: chicken pox, or varicella virus, on rare occasions kills otherwise healthy adults. I caught it, though no one knows how. The virus first attacked my lungs, then inflamed my spinal cord and entered my brain. Once it had run its course, it left my diaphragm paralyzed. I could not breathe at all on my own. I was kept alive by a life support system.

Then, the opportunistic and sometimes drug-resistant pneumonia bacteria that lurk in every hospital began their assaults. I went into a coma that lasted three months while the doctors fought and defeated one infection after another. But each attack weakened me and increased the danger not only of crippling brain damage but that my kidneys or heart or lungs would suddenly fail. On several occasions my wife was warned that everything that could be done medically had been done, and that I might not survive the night, unless that mysterious human quality called "will" brought me through.

The coma visions and close encounters with death in this novel are described exactly as I experienced them. I suspect I will always be haunted by them, just as I probably shall always have to walk with a cane.

But you never know what Signore Destino has in mind. Although I may sometimes fall as I'm walking, I can always get up and keep going. And I'm able to do what I love most—writing stories.

What Bruno's Signore Destino taught me is simple but powerful. The dailiness of life means very little, the career successes and failures are insignificant. The only things that truly count are our human relationships, the resilience of the spirit of life we all possess, and our capacity for love.

I'd be dead—and I am absolutely convinced of this—without the love and the supporting spirit of my wife, my family and friends, my doctors and nurses and aides.

Beyond the technology, the wonder drugs, the CAT and MIR machines, they all willed me to survive. And Signore Destino approved their efforts.

I hope he'll approve of what I do with my second chance.

Thomas Moran divides his time between Woodstock and Europe with his wife and son. He is also the author of *The Man in the Box*. His novels have been translated into five languages.